Coffee, Tea or Mr. ___?
Why your date is like
your favorite drink.

1. We know you'd never do it, but fess up—haven't you met at least *one* person you'd like to grind up (or cut up into tiny pieces) and boil?

2. The intense and exotic *seem* attractive, but wouldn't you rather face something simple and trustworthy first thing in the morning for the rest of your life?

3. It doesn't matter where or when you see him—you're obnoxious and grumpy before, but energized and happier after.

4. Eleanor Roosevelt had it right: the best way to really know what someone is made of is to see what they do in hot water.

Books by Allie Pleiter

Love Inspired

My So-Called Love Life #359
The Perfect Blend #405

Steeple Hill Books

Bad Heiress Day
Queen Esther & the Second Graders of Doom

ALLIE PLEITER

Enthusiastic but slightly untidy mother of two, Allie Pleiter writes both fiction and nonfiction. An avid knitter and unreformed chocoholic, she spends her days writing books, drinking coffee and finding new ways to avoid housework. Allie grew up in Connecticut, holds a B.S. in speech from Northwestern University and spent fifteen years in the field of professional fundraising. She lives with her husband, children and a Havanese dog named Bella in the suburbs of Chicago, Illinois.

The Perfect Blend
Allie Pleiter

Steeple
Hill®

Published by Steeple Hill Books™

STEEPLE HILL BOOKS

Steeple
Hill®

ISBN-13: 978-0-373-87441-5
ISBN-10:   0-373-87441-3

THE PERFECT BLEND

Copyright © 2007 by Alyse Stanko Pleiter

www.SteepleHill.com

Printed in U.S.A.

Lord, you have assigned me my portion
and my cup; you have made my lot secure.

The boundary lines have fallen
for me in pleasant places; surely I have
a delightful inheritance.

—*Psalms* 16:5-6

To Patrick & Donna
May God grant you a long and
wonderful life together

This book was the "perfect blend" of many hearts and minds. Thanks to Ellie Hudson-Matuszak at Intellegentsia Coffee Roasters for lending both her passion and expertise in coffee. Tony Goodhew and Todd Gaiser provided a highly entertaining crash course in rugby. Ann Roth, Dawn Kinzer, Annette Irby and Evelyn Ray lent Seattle insight and hospitality. Leanne Larkin at the Hill House Bed and Breakfast served as my Seattle "home base," putting up with endless odd questions. My education in Asian tea ceremonies came from the Urasenke Foundation Seattle Branch and from Regina at The Tea Box in Denver, Colorado. Sue McCown at Earth & Ocean offered food and dining inspirations, not to mention one killer chocolate dessert. Each of you—along with many others—made this work a delightful experience. To my friends and family, thanks again for keeping me sane and grounded (pun intended!) while God worked yet another of His wonders through my fingertips. I'm grateful to you all.

Chapter One

No?

"No."

No? No?

He said no. Well, *they* said no. *They* being the bank, *no* being "we won't give you a loan."

His English accent did not soften the blow. This loan is step one to realizing my God-given dream. My purpose on earth. The reason God put me here. So, it stands to reason that I am not supposed to hear "no." That's not the way it works, is it?

I twist my handbag strap between my hands. "No?" I counter, attempting calm despite the ice-water shock that just doused me. "Just like that, 'no.' Not 'based on current trends in the beverage industry.'" As my nerves tense, my eyes shift around the cool tones of this all-too-corporate office. Steel door, glass panels, chrome hardware. It feels far too tight, too rigid in here.

And him? He's crisp and courteous, seated behind a large desk of blond wood and yet more chrome. Surrounded by neatly stacked files. With typed labels and color coding. The picture of efficiency. His pencils line up. Even his smooth blond hair looks as though it wouldn't dare disobey orders. I cannot go to pieces in front of someone this executive-ish, even if he looks like he's barely older than I am.

"Just 'no.'" I repeat, my jaw tightening.

William Grey—the *third,* no less, according to his big shiny nameplate on his big shiny desk— arches a blond eyebrow at me. "Would you have preferred something less direct?"

I do prefer directness. But I prefer direct positives, not direct rejections. They did actually read my loan request, didn't they? I spent two *whole* weeks filling out their endless quadruplicate paperwork, laying out my dream to open a Christian coffeehouse in excruciating detail.

I resist the urge to stand and plant my hands on his desk. "You guys did actually read my application, didn't you? This is an educated 'no'?" Direct, maybe, but that loan application was mighty compelling reading if you ask me. For years I've bumped around my life, taking this job and that, never finding what it was I was really meant to do. Then God flooded my brain with the idea one day last year and the world fell into place. My own personal burning bush, humming in every fiber of my being, driving me from that day forward with an irresistible force. Who could say no to something so important?

Mr. Grey looks perplexed. Like a man collecting his thoughts to attempt an explanation of particle physics to preschoolers. "Us guys," he mimics, the phrase sounding ludicrous in his accent, "do our homework on small-business loans. As a matter of fact, Miss Black," he continues, holding up a file with the typed label Black, Margaret, "I read your application myself. We do read them, you know. Carefully. It's not as if we sit atop a stack of money and flip coins to see which loans we grant." Should I worry that I'm color-coded red? Is that a good thing or a bad thing? Red could mean urgent or it could mean stop.

Based on that last comment, it might mean stop. Ouch! And here I was hoping Mr. William Grey III was actually a nice guy. He does have a velvety English accent that would sound so lovely saying the words, "Of course, Miss Black, we'd be delighted to loan you the money to open your coffeehouse."

He's not saying that, though, is he? No, I've got someone out of Charles Dickens telling me he won't be handing me the money I need.

I clear my throat, ordering the lump inside to rise no further. "Can you at least tell me *why* you're saying no?"

"*I'm* not saying no, Miss Black, the bank is."

I roll my eyes, my disappointment getting the best of me. "What's the difference?"

He leans forward. "Believe it or not, it makes a rather big difference in this case. Are you willing to hear me out?"

Behind me I hear the click of computer keyboards and hushed voices on telephones, the wheels of efficient, soulless commerce turning all around me. I just nod, even though what I want to say is: "You've got all the money. Do I have a choice?" *Okay, Maggie, try to rein in the supreme disappointment and act like a rational adult here.*

"Excellent choice," he replies to my nod. "Now, loosen that stranglehold you currently have on your handbag, take a deep breath and listen to what I'm about to propose."

The beige walls still insist on closing in. Ever have one of those high-emotion moments where your sense of humor fires up for all the wrong reasons? You know—weddings, funerals, bank rejections, first kisses, that sort of thing? Happens to me all the time. So, right now, my tension-fed sense of humor is misbehaving and decides to land on tea. As in Earl Grey tea. And suddenly I'm sitting in front of "Earl Grey" and that's just too funny. A small laugh erupts from me before I can stop it.

His lordship—oh dear, where did that come from?—widens his blue eyes. "Have I said something amusing, Miss Black?"

You'd think that by now I'd have learned never to try and explain my weird sense of humor. "No, really, it's just…" I notice the bland still life hanging behind his lordship, which *of course* contains a teapot, and the chuckle mutates into a jerky, nervous laugh. *Come on, Maggie, pull it together.* "No, you've said nothing that's…" I can't help myself. I'm laughing and he's staring and this is going downhill fast. I imagine heads popping up over cubicle walls behind me like a field of prairie dogs.

"Are you quite all right?" His expression is somewhere between amusement and concern.

"Oh, no, I'm…fine. Well, not really, since you turned down my loan, but I mean…." I put my hand up in a just-give-me-a-minute gesture, which thankfully sends him over to his credenza for a glass of water.

Mr. Grey sets the water in front of me and sits down. Oh, no, he's doing that thing. That thing where men close their eyes and pinch the bridge of their nose. That I-don't-want-to-deal-with-this-right-now expression. "Might we attempt a conversation, Miss Black?"

I take a deep breath. "Yes, of course. I'm sorry. Nerves, I guess." I'm giggling again and drown any further reply in a deep swallow of water.

"Why don't we try a visual?" he suggests, letting out a slightly exasperated sigh. Reaching down, he produces a Seattle Yellow Pages. "Would you like to look up 'coffee' or shall I?"

I take the thick book from his hands and flip through to the pages marked Coffee Shops and Retail Coffee Dealers.

It's not hard to find. There are fifteen pages of them. I think I'm getting his point.

"Would you agree with me that coffeehouses rather abound in this city?"

"None like mine," I fire back. What do you know? Getting my dander up is the surest way to squelch my nerves.

"Would you like to know how many times I hear that exact sentiment?" He steeples his hands and I notice a thick, intricate school ring on his finger. Oxford? Cambridge? He does have a high-achieving, valedictorian air about him. Just the kind of hard-nosed realist to hand me eighty reasons why a Christian coffeehouse is too big a risk in a city already jam-packed with java joints.

"But my coffeehouse is different. It really is," I snap back a bit too sharply. I'm in no mood to hear his version of the Seattle-has-enough-coffeehouses speech. I've heard it dozens of times. But God doesn't really need to care about rationales like that. He's God. What He says goes.

Grey looks at me intently. His eyes are almost too dark to be called blue; they're more like a blend of blue and gray. His face, although sharp-featured, has too much warmth in it to be completely heartless. He's actually trying to be nice, I think. Trying, but not really succeeding.

"An astounding number of small businesses fail in their first year. The rates are higher amongst restaurants. The rates in an already saturated market are…"

"Of no interest to me," I cut in, trying not to sound frustrated. "I'm *supposed* to do this. I *know* I am. I'm not even asking you for a lot of money, I've already got more than half of what I need."

"With all respect, I don't think you know half of what you need, Miss Black."

Wait a minute—is he telling me I'm not smart enough to open a coffeehouse? "What do you…"

"Miss Black, *will you let me finish?*" His eyes shoot to the glass panel behind me, where I'm guessing heads really are popping up over cubicle walls.

"Will you please consider the fact that *no* might just mean not yet?" He takes a breath, softening his tone. "The bank runs a small-business incubator— an entrepreneur school, if you will—for loan applicants with promising ideas but insufficient training."

"Entrepreneur school?" I don't like the sound of this at all.

"It's a twelve-week small-business-administration course. Your loan application fee becomes your tuition and you come out of the course with a five-year small-business plan."

Twelve weeks? Of school? Wasn't the first sixteen years enough? Granted, it was a sociology degree, but I remember taking math in there somewhere.

As if sensing my doubts, Mr. Grey adds, "You also have your loan reevaluated. With a much higher chance of approval."

I narrow one eye. "So if I go to school for three months you'll give me my money?"

Something almost like a smile crosses his face. "Well, no, I'm not saying that. I'm saying you stand a much greater chance of getting your money." He hands me a thick envelope.

I picture myself slumped behind a desk, doodling on a syllabus while some retired banker drones on about compound interest and healthy earnings ratios. I can't brew a blend strong enough to keep me awake for that. "Who teaches this course?"

He wipes his hand down his face. "As a matter of fact, I do."

You know, he's making an effort here. It could be he's really not such a bad guy—for a banker. A little tight around the edges, but appealing in a distinguished, Jane Eyre kind of way. The accent alone could get me through Accounting 101. Add a triple-shot caramel-hazelnut latte and I just might survive. I force a cooperative smile. "And who reevaluates my loan and the prize-winning business plan I'll have when I'm done?"

"I do."

Near as I can tell, His lordship holds all the cards. Or, in this case, all the cash.

I'm impulsive, visionary and a bit rebellious, but I'm not stupid. I hold out my hand.

"Mr. Grey, you're on."

I know a fair trade when I see one. If it gets my coffeehouse open, I can endure twelve weeks of anybody.

Right?

Chapter Two

Right?

Wrong.

I needed a wheelbarrow to get my books and manuals home from the first class. *Professor* Grey seems to think we don't have anything better to do with our daylight hours than read textbooks. Hoards of textbooks.

We've got class again on Wednesday and when I return to that austere little classroom on the fourth floor of the First Bank building, I'm bringing coffee. The stuff out of the vending machine could barely be called a liquid, much less a coffee. Not only that, but it's part of my homework. Since Mr. Grey seems to enjoy visuals and we are supposed to bring in a description of what makes our business distinct from its competition, I'm going for the real thing. Refreshments are definitely in order. Can't you just smell an A brewing here?

"Mags? You still in there?" My best friend Diane raps on my head lightly. She's helping me buy jeans for my brother John. John is just one of my three brothers—there are five of us Black kids, in case you were wondering. Now I know what you're thinking: men's jeans, two-minute acquisition, right? Not for John, which is why I brought Diane. John's a clothing fanatic. Must have the coolest of the coolest. This might be to compensate for the hair: every single one of us is topped off with a head of unruly auburn curls. If you want a picture of the quintessential large Irish family, just line us up.

Since I got stuck handling the siblings' birthday presents for John (with five of us we've learned to trade off), I need Diane's talent for choosing trendy clothing. I had sent her after four pairs while I had cozied up with *Basic Concepts in Marketing*.

Diane taps the textbook with her free hand and I look up as she shows off her stack of jeans. Diane is blessed with razor-straight brown hair, doe eyes and a model's figure, so she needn't have such a keen sense of style—she looks great in everything. She's the girl next door you wish really did live next door. "Looks juicy." She squints over the complex graph I'm deciphering.

"It's boring, but necessary. Am I done yet?"

Diane smiles. "You and your fellow offspring are all set."

"No, we're all broke," I correct her. "Have you seen how much the jeans are in this place? If John would only let me take him to the secondhand stores…."

"He'd be you," Diane counters. "Happy birthday to John from you," she says, laying a pair of jeans over my textbook. She piles on the rest. "And from Cathy, Steve and Luke."

"So now, all I do is pay these ridiculous prices and then get Cathy, Steve and Luke to pay up. When did I become loan officer for the First Bank of Black Siblings?"

This remark, mind you, proves my theory that I am spending way too much time thinking about high finance these days. It's unnatural for live, vibrant human beings to spend so much of their energy on numbers. Art, love, faith, joy—these are the pursuits worth chasing. I don't even think money's worth chasing, unless it's as a means to an end. Nicely behaving calculations? Not my thing.

But definitely his lordship's thing. As I stack up my purchases and fork over the unnatural sum required for four cool jeans, I think about William Grey's obvious love of numbers. I thought I was signing up for a twelve-week stint of boredom, but he is actually trying to make it interesting. Which is, of course, a losing battle—I'd guess ninety percent of the class is there under the same loan blackmail I'm enduring. But this guy's fascination with the subject is…well…compelling. I don't remember the equation he was teaching, but what

I do remember is the line he drew when he summed it up. A precise, energetic line that he spread across the whiteboard like a knight drawing a sword. Really, that's what it looked like to me. Gallant math? I admit, it's a stretch, but I'd swear that's how William Grey sees it. As if he's a valiant knight leading us all on a crusade to sound business practices. The man has more fun with math than *I'd* ever think possible.

And that gets me wondering. Could someone that efficiency-minded grasp God's economy? I know Christian bankers exist. I've never met one, but they've got to be out there. Maybe I'll invite him to discuss tithing over lattes once I've got my place open.

"So, have you told your parents?" Diane asks as we make our way to the car. Diane is the only person in the world I've told about my plans.

"No. I'm waiting for the right time."

Diane snickers. "There's no right time to tell your dad you're dumping your money into a coffeehouse. Even a Christian coffeehouse. You know that."

"Thanks, Einstein." I nod toward the jeans. "Dad already told John if he does anything other than go to college with Uncle Ian's money, he'll be chopped up into little pieces and told never to come home again."

"Well, it's good advice." Diane says, applying her big sister voice. "College is important."

"Uncle Ian's words were, *For each Black child to use to fulfill God's purpose in their life.*" The phrase has gotten a bit of use since Uncle Ian gave each of us Black kids a tidy sum of money last year, along with his admonition to use it for God's glory. Uncle Ian is, by Dad's standards, far wealthier than he is wise. He made a killing in some computer-chip thing, got in a car accident, then gave most of it away and went to live on an island off Jamaica to write the great American Christian novel.

You can imagine how nuts this made Dad. He and Mom got their own little pot of fun money, too, that Dad promptly socked into municipal something-things without indulging in so much as a steak dinner.

John, by the way, is thinking that God would be best glorified by an electric guitar and a new van— both apparently necessary for his garage band. Ah, high school.

I can't really talk, though, can I? I'm pretty sure Dad's going to have a tough time swallowing the concept that God is best glorified in my life by a missionary mint mocha.

Still, when I picture Higher Grounds—that's the name I've already chosen for my business—I can see it clear as day. A place where faith is hip and relevant. The coolest spot ever for your singles bible study. Filled with color and sound and deep conversation. Walls crammed with great books and CDs that reinvent contemporary Christian music. Definitely *not* your mother's prayer circle. Filled with funky mosaic tables and overstuffed chairs, with plenty of nooks and corners to hold great discussions. A showcase for rising local talent. And the best coffee this side of the pearly gates.

Coffee's a way to reach souls, I tell you. Especially in this town. Coffee's my gift, my talent, my mission outreach. I want to brew coffee so fab that nonbelievers will put up with (and eventually be influenced by) the faith element, just to score the best cappuccino in town. They'll keep coming back and I'll keep telling them about faith and, bit by bit, God will do His thing in their hearts while I do my thing in their mugs.

I can see every detail of the place when I close my eyes. Right down to the napkins.

Now you see why I don't need a five-year plan. I've already got one, clear as day, from God.

Chapter Three

If you brew it…

If this is the birthplace of business, it's no cuddly nursery. For all the creative minds they expect to be gathering in this room, launching exciting new businesses and inventing spectacular new products, they didn't give a thought to the power of environment. This place is drab.

Steel chairs cue up in neat lines on a thin carpet the color of granite surrounded by off-white, windowless walls. My high school chemistry lab had more personality. I feel as though I'm inhaling the blandness of this place every minute I sit through class.

Tonight, though, is my chance to bring a little spark into this world. I hoist my bright red cup, complete with its mock-up of my company logo—coffee beans arranged in the Christian *ichthus* fish symbol—and toast the class. The smell of freshly brewed coffee fills the room. Each bland gray desk now boasts a cup of coffee and a cherry cheesecake square resting on a bright red napkin. Soft "mmms" murmur through the classroom as nodding faces lick lips.

"Because, you see, it's the excellence and consistency of the brew, combined with an irresistible atmosphere, that will build a solid customer base. Location will be important, but brand loyalty is key to the coffee customer. Tell me, how many of you have a favorite coffeehouse?" All hands shoot up, except for—and you knew this one was coming— "professor" Grey back there filling his notebook with comments on my presentation. He leans back and crosses his arms across his chest. "And how often do you go elsewhere?" I ask. The class shrugs their shoulders and a few wag their heads—a general consensus that, all things being equal, no one likes to go elsewhere.

Theory confirmed. Coffee brewed. Assignment aced. From the looks of it, I've got half the class ready to plunk down their money right now and I haven't said one word about God, Jesus or the irresistible power of the Holy Spirit and brilliant espresso. You're looking at a living, breathing, no-fail java-for-Jesus campaign.

Mr. Grey clears his throat. "I must admit, Miss Black, you do craft a compelling pitch—even if I do prefer tea myself. I trust your paper is as inspired as your beverage service?"

Tea? Paper? But he said to *demonstrate* how our

businesses would be distinct. For my business, that can't be put on paper—it gets poured into cups. I put it in the class's cups. And they drank it. No, they *downed* it like the liquid gold it is. "This demonstration is my paper. You asked us to demonstrate our business's unique qualities. I'm demonstrating. Do I really need the other kind?"

Uh-oh. The furrowing eyebrow tells me Mr. Grey meant demonstrate *on paper.* And here I thought I'd taken the spirit of the assignment and gone one step further to demonstrate the very soul of my business.

"Yes," he says slowly, "you do."

"How you get customers into a coffeehouse is great coffee. That's the marketing. That's the advertising. There's no complicated planning involved. This is Seattle. Even the *preschoolers* understand the concept of coffeehouses in this town."

"My assignment was a four-page marketing plan for your first eighteen months of operation demonstrating the unique niche of your business."

"And you're drinking it." Okay, he's the only one *not* drinking it, but I think he gets my point.

"I admit I may need to rethink my choice of verbs in the future, but I did quite clearly assign a *paper.* A paper, I'm now reasonably sure, you did not write." There goes that eyebrow again.

"Mr. Grey…"

"I'd like to see you after class, Miss Black."

"But Mr. Grey…"

"We'll discuss this *after class,* Miss Black."

Ice. The air in here just dropped twenty-five degrees. This guy doesn't just teach a class, he commands it.

"Now," he says, the civility instantly returning to his voice, "Mr. Davis, let's hear your paper on your gourmet pasta-sauce line. I trust there's no fettuccine involved?" How'd he turn off the ice so quickly? How'd he do that in two sentences?

Jerry Davis, aspiring king of the Daviccio Pasta Sauce empire, rises from his seat. Actually, *king* might be overstating things. Jerry's a small, round fellow. A nervous, shy man who acts as if he wants to be friendly but can't quite work up the nerve. Round bald head, round glasses, round build. You know the type—the one guy so continually overlooked that he's almost convinced he's invisible? I have a heart for the Jerrys of this world. If Jerry could realize God loves him as much as the perfect, macho types, he'd gain some of the confidence he needs. God could do wonders with the tender heart I'm guessing is hiding under all that insecurity. But, like all the other Jerry-types I've met, he's probably too shy to venture into a strange church.

I could get him into my coffee bar, though, I'm sure of it. Higher Grounds is just the place for guys like Jerry.

"No," Jerry replies in a small, unsteady voice, "but I did bring a mock-up of the package label. I hope that's okay? Nothing inside, it's just a model. I didn't cook anything. I wasn't supposed to cook anything, was I?"

"No, you weren't," assures Mr. Grey, who has also tried to bolster Jerry's in-class confidence. "Let's just hear your paper."

"Good coffee," Jerry whispers to me as he takes tiny, rolling steps up the aisle to the class podium. It does not help my disposition, as you might imagine. Poor Jerry, I don't hear his presentation. I spend the rest of class thinking about *Professor Earl Grey*, my botched assignment and what's going to happen after class. This guy gets under my skin far too fast. I obviously misunderstood the assignment (or maybe took it one step further, depending on how you look at it). I shouldn't be this annoyed.

If self-control is a fruit of the Spirit, I need a couple of bushels to descend on me over the next forty minutes or…

Or we won't think about that. Breathe. Sip my coffee. Breathe. Sip. Try to listen to the nice pasta man talk about plum tomatoes….

"Please, have a seat." Ever polite, William Grey sets down my box full of coffee, cups and carafes. I notice a few more details in the office—I think they were always there but I was just too nervous to see them. There's a plant in the far corner. Two trophies—football maybe?—huddle on one corner of his credenza. There's a map of England on one wall.

Now that I think about it, the Earl Grey joke isn't really far off the mark. William Grey III is the kind of guy who would stand when you left the restaurant table and open your car door for you—part of an endangered species, really. He's got a lot of class, so even if he plans to chew me out, chances are he'll be civil about it.

"Thanks," I say, "Look, I…"

"Please," he interjects, holding up a hand while he reaches down to pull open a desk drawer, "let me do the talking this time. I believe you need to see this. It seems you are the kind of person who needs a visual."

Is that an insult? The way he said it, I'm not sure.

To my surprise, he holds out a tin of brownies. "Taste these." Brownies? What's that got to do with anything?

"I don't get it."

"Humor me, Miss Black. Taste these."

I botch the assignment and he offers me chocolate-laden baked goods? I take one and nibble off a corner.

My nibble quickly inflates into a full-fledged chomp. It's one fine brownie. I mean *really* fine. It walks the delicate balance of gooey and cakey, of held together and melt-in-your-mouth. Wow. There's some special flavor in there, something I've never tasted in a brownie before. Cinnamon? Maple? I'm not sure, but it's wonderful. Hands down the best brownie I've ever tasted and I don't hand out baked-goods compliments lightly.

He breaks off a corner of one from the tin and puts it in his mouth. He takes the briefest of moments to savor it. It's odd to watch—it's not a business face at all, but an out-of-place expression of enjoyment. After a moment, he smiles.

Oh, my. That smile belongs on a pirate, not a banker. Smooth, bright, and not at all what I'd expect on William Grey III. He'd better not do that too often, or I might have to start liking him.

"Splendid, isn't it?"

"Um, yes. That's a really good brownie."

"I'd venture to say it's the best brownie in Seattle."

"I was thinking it's the best brownie I've ever tasted."

"I'd agree." He snaps the lid on the tin with a precise click. I take another bite. *Splendid* is definitely the word for it. I should get these in my coffeehouse—I'd walk ten blocks out of my way in high heels for these. "They filed for bankruptcy this morning."

"Huh?" I say. *With* my mouth full of brownie, too shocked to remember my table manners.

"Tortoise Bakeries. Maker of outstanding goodies such as these brownies. Top-notch stuff. They filed for bankruptcy this morning."

"Oh."

"I could tell you dozens of stories like this one, but I think you need concrete evidence. Would you not agree this is one—what's that word you use?— 'fab' brownie?"

"It's terrific." I don't like where this is heading.

"It's *not enough.* What I'm trying to get you to grasp, Miss Black, is that outstanding product simply isn't enough. The world's best brownie will not keep a company afloat if no one knows about it. Word of mouth is powerful, I'll grant you that, but you cannot build your business on it. Not while you're paying rent and staff and buying supplies. This is not a case of if you brew it they will come."

"Mr. Grey, you possess a sense of humor!"

"Miss Black, *have* I made my point?"

God, in His infinite wisdom, sent me a banker who argues using baked goods. Like I said earlier, I'm rebellious, but I'm not stupid. "Okay, fine, I think I'd better write that paper."

His smile ignites again. "I knew you'd come round. Excellent. You've got twenty-four hours to turn it in. Actually," he says, checking his watch—his very nice watch but I'm not noticing or anything—"more like twenty. I'll expect it on my desk by 5:00 p.m. tomorrow."

"What? You're kidding!"

"You'll find I rarely joke, Miss Black."

So much for his sense of humor. "I've got to work tomorrow. I'll be up all night to get it done."

"Good thing you have plenty of excellent coffee on hand."

"You can't!"

"I'm extending you a favor, Miss Black. I'd take it if I were you."

How does he sound so civil and so mean at the same time? But what can I do? His lordship holds all the cards.

"All right." I shoot off my chair, snatch up my box of supplies and apply every ounce of will I possess not to say something nasty. "It'll be on your desk by 5:00 p.m. tomorrow, Mr. Grey. If you'll excuse me, it seems I have a whopping load of work to do."

"Miss Black?"

I drag myself back around to face him. "What?"

"You do make excellent coffee."

Yeah? Well, I'm gonna need it, aren't I?

Chapter Four

Toads and rugby

I fell asleep over my paper at 2:15 a.m. Still, I thought, I just might make it. Until I remembered the toad.

Not just any toad, my nephew, Charlie the toad. More precisely, Charlie's mom, my sister Cathy, whom I promised, in a fit of virtuous auntmanship, that I would come see Charlie in his toad costume. Today is Charlie's vacation Bible school play, The Wetlands, God's Delicate Treasure, and as his aunt and godmother I have-have-have to be there. I've seen the script. Cathy and I didn't privately rename it *Habitats for Insanity* for nothing. It would have been hard to stay awake through it on a full night's sleep, much less the night I just had.

So, surrendering to the enormous pressures surrounding me at every turn, I called in sick to my afternoon shift at the flower shop where I work and spent half the morning applauding a toad.

And the printer malfunction at 2:25 p.m.? Let's not even go there.

All of which is a rather lengthy explanation as to why I am currently sprinting down Thirty-Fifth Avenue. Racing the clock, highly nonathletic sandals in one hand and paper in the other, to get myself through the bank doors by 5:00 p.m.

At 5:10 I hop through the lobby, bending over sideways to get my last shoe back on, and skid to a halt outside William Grey's office door.

William Grey's dark, *locked* office door.

Oh, come on. Who actually gets to leave their job at five anymore? Even in banking?

"You must be Miss Black," says a female voice behind me. I turn to see a woman who could be everybody's grandmother looking at me from over a stack of files. "He waited as long as he could, but you just missed him." She has a face that should be behind a plate of oven-fresh biscuits, not a pile of papers.

I slump against the wall and nearly strangle my paper. "So close."

"And you ran all the way here from the looks of it. That's a shame." For a moment I thought she was going to say *dearie* at the end of her sentence. I *have* been up too long. She motions toward her desk at the end of the hallway

"It's a shame all right," I mutter. "A big, fat, sad turn of events, that's what it is."

Grandma Biscuits applies a *let's just pretend you*

didn't say that look to her face and offers me a chair. "Can I get you a glass of water?" she says, setting down her files. She's dressed in one of those knit suits all older women seem to wear and she looks at me over bright silver half-moon spectacles.

"Does it come with a few thousand dollars in start-up funding?"

"No, but it could come with ice." Her charm bracelet rattles as she holds up a single finger. "And a little useful information." She bustles off to the water cooler and returns with ice water. "Bea Haversham," she says, extending her hand along with the glass. "You must be Margaret Black."

"Maggie. Thanks." I take the water. "Formerly of the small-business incubator program."

"The coffee lady." She chuckles and shakes her head. "I have to say, that was one of the more interesting applications we've had in quite a while." She peeks at me from over the top of her glasses. "You're not one for filling out forms, are you?"

I down the water. "You read my loan application?"

"I read them all. How else could I pull the files together correctly?" She hands me a tissue from a needlepoint-covered box on her desk. "You're perspiring, dear."

"I just ran from the auxiliary parking lot. I'm lucky I'm still breathing." I wipe my forehead and stare at my paper. "For all the good it did me."

Bea cranes her head over the edge of her desk to look at my feet. "You ran from the auxiliary parking lot—in *those* shoes—to turn in this paper?"

"The sprint to the finish line was not part of the original plan."

"Well, now," she says, taking back the empty water glass and handing me another tissue, "I think we simply must take that into consideration here. You'd have made it well under the wire had you been in a pair of sensible shoes. And been able to park closer to the bank. Honestly, I've got senior customers who'll turn around and go home before they make the three-block trek from the auxiliary parking lot. I've told Will we need a shuttle bus. And you, honey, look at you. Have you got any blisters? Do you need a bandage?"

She looks like one of those people who has everything you'd need—ever—in the bottom drawer of her desk. "No, really, I'm okay. I just tried to run too fast. Just give me a minute and I'll be okay."

"I'll do better than that. I'll give you eleven minutes and an alibi." Bea gives me a wink and reaches into the candy jar on the other corner of her desk. She pulls out a fistful of peppermints and calls out in a melodic voice, "Oh, Hal? Hal dear, could you come here for a moment?"

I sit perfectly still, baffled by this twist of events.

Hal, who looks like he walked off the set of *Mayberry RFD*, saunters over with his thumbs tucked in his belt loops. "Whassup, Mizz Haversham?"

Bea presses the candies into Hal's beefy palm with an air of pure conspiracy. "You didn't realize you gave Miss Black here the wrong directions now, did you?"

"Huh?"

"When she came in to give her paper to Mr. Grey a few minutes ago. You gave her directions to the upstairs conference room because you thought Will was up there, didn't you?" She puts her hand back in the candy jar and rustles around enticingly in the cellophane wrappers.

"I did?"

"And it was 4:48 when you did it, wasn't it?"

Hal's eyes shift from side to side, straining to follow her lead. "Well...I..."

"I'm quite certain. It's *our fault* Miss Black didn't make her deadline. We'll have to do something to set things right, won't we?"

Hal gives up. "Sure, Bea, whatever you say."

Bea hands him three more candies. "You just let me handle everything. I'll see to it that Miss Black gets her paper where it needs to go. Bless you for being such a dear, Hal. I always know I can count on you."

I'm now officially at a complete loss for words. However, Bea Haversham has just won herself a lifetime of free coffee when my shop opens.

"Sweet boy," she whispers to me. "Now, let's get you settled." She opens her top drawer to fetch a notepad. "Mr. Grey's playing rugby at Sand Point," she writes down the address of a nearby park. She leans in toward me. "I think he'd have actually stayed and waited for you if it weren't a game day. They'll be the fellows in the blue-and-yellow shirts. 'Course, you already know what a handsome fellow

Will is so you'll have no trouble at all finding him.
Head on over there when they break between halves
which should be," she checks her watch, "in about
ten minutes." She gives me another wink. "I'll back
you up all the way."

I don't know what to say. "Bea Haversham,
you're an answer to prayer."

She waves me away in a rattle of charms. "So I
keep hearing from Will. Now scoot or you'll have
to wait until the game is over."

Huge. This park is huge. Where'd she say they
play again? I've been to three parking lots and I
have yet to find the…the what? Field? Pitch? What
actually is rugby anyway? I only know it's something manly English guys play involving a ball and
lots of mud.

Finally, following the sound of men yelling, I
find them up over a hill behind the tennis courts. I
encounter a small army of grungy, grunting men,
hurling themselves at each other over an egg-
shaped ball. Blue-and-yellow striped shirts slam
into green-and-gray striped shirts, but I have no
idea who's winning. From the intensity on the field,
however, I'm certain they're keeping score. These
guys look out for blood.

So this is rugby. William Grey III plays this?
I'm a bit stunned; this doesn't really look like the
kind of pastime ultra-tailored Earl Grey would get
into.

Just as I'm ten yards or so from the blue-and-yellow sideline of the field, the whistle blows. Bea knows her stuff. Men jog off to their respective sidelines, chug bottles of water and toss each other numerous ice packs. Only half of them even bother to wipe the mud off their faces with grimy towels. Blood, mud and testosterone: it looks like a living macho deodorant ad.

I spot Grey in a heartbeat. Which is a good way to put it, because he looks shockingly different from the usual Mr. Grey. Talk about your hundred and eighty-degree turns. He's in a striped shirt with a swath of mud down one sleeve, a pair of black shorts, mud-soaked socks and even muddier shoes.

The biggest shock of all, however, is how he looks. Most guys look rugged when dirty, hitting truly handsome when you clean them up. William Grey, on the other hand, goes from dashing to downright dangerous when you get him out of that suit coat.

I remind myself just how inappropriate that thought is, that I know nothing of the personality, spirituality or even the rationality of William Grey III. I take a deep breath and walk calmly toward him. Which isn't as easy as it looks, especially with my heels sinking into the turf with each step.

"Mr. Grey?"

He looks up from a water jug, his eyes wide when he recognizes me. "Miss Black?"

"Ms. Haversham sent me over. I didn't find you at the bank when I came to deliver the paper." That's not a lie. I don't lie, but I do admit it took me the whole drive over to come up with a non-condemning truthful statement.

I watch him try and reconcile facts. Evidently Bea is as good as her word, for he walks toward me with his hand out. "You're determined, I'll grant you that. But you'll find I am rather serious about my deadlines." Some of his teammates start buzzing around behind him, shouting, tossing the ball back and forth, gearing up for the next half.

I don't have much time. "I came to the bank and she…"

The world goes completely, instantly black.

Chapter Five

One way to get an A...

Pain.

The most pain I have felt, ever. An enormous boulder has just slammed into my face, breaking it into a million screaming pieces. Explosions go off behind my eyes and the ground comes up behind me until I am curled sideways on the wet grass, clutching at my face, howling.

"Sumners, you great lumbering oaf!" It's a voice I dimly recognize, seeming to come from miles away. My hands are wet, my face is wet, I can barely pull in enough breath to fuel my gasps of pain. There is a hand on my shoulder, trying to pull me upright but I remain curled in agony. I want to swat the large hand away, but I refuse to move either hand from my exploding face. "Miss Black? Miss Black, can you hear me?"

Some part of me recognizes the voice. "Owwww."

"I'll assume that is a yes." From out of the darkness something rough and moist comes up against my hands. "This is a towel and ice. Come now, you'll need it."

Through the pain's fog, my female side registers that I must look pretty awful based on the number of bodies I sense standing around me. I have enough brothers to know nothing draws attention like a gruesome injury. With a sticky sadness I realize the wetness on my hands and face is blood. I've broken my nose. Or my eyes. Or both. Can you break your eyes? My current pain level says oh, yes, definitely.

The voice comes into the fog again. "You could be seriously hurt. Let me have a look at you."

"No." I reply, half whining, half crying. I attempt to upright myself, with poor results. The world keeps spinning under me.

"No time to be brave, Miss Black. You've had quite a knock. You're most definitely hurt."

I pry one eye open to peek at Mr. Grey from between my bloodied fingers. With my tiny slice of vision I snatch the towel from his hand, careful to keep the other hand over my throbbing face. I feel as though I've just had all my teeth polished by a jackhammer.

"Yes," Grey says as he gestures his burly team-mates to back away, "I do believe that's our Miss Black in there somewhere." He comes closer and softens his voice. "All right then, up with you. If you don't sit up we'll never get that bleeding to stop."

"I…"

A set of arms scoops me up without any further ado and I find myself unable to stop them. I'm too dizzy, for starters, and I'm using both my hands to hold the ice and towel on my face. In that weird detachment that comes with an injury or accident, I wonder just how clean this towel is. Am I stemming blood loss or facilitating infection?

"What hit me?" I moan as I am deposited on a picnic table bench. Gentle hands guide my elbow onto the table so I can slump against it and achieve some semblance of verticality. I feel him pull the stray hair out of my face and touch my hands and arms, testing for further injuries. The explosions of pain have dulled into a tremendous sense of pressure, as if my face were swelling up like a beach ball.

Which, I'm guessing, isn't far from the truth. I'm already having to breathe through my mouth because my nose feels like it's the size of a potato.

"Arthur Sumners, who has just seriously jeopardized his standing as my best mate, hit you with a ball."

I run a tongue over what feels like bulging split lip. I must look like I was in a brawl. "Ball of what? Concrete?"

He manages a chuckle, reaching behind him for a new towel some teammate just handed him. "Rugby balls aren't exactly soft, it pains me to say." He holds out his hand, gesturing for me to swap the clean (and I use that word loosely) towel for the one on my face.

"Pains *you?*" I'm about to continue when the sheer volume of blood on the towel I hold sends the world spinning again. "Oh…"

I feel Mr. Grey's hand catch me as I slump forward. "And that would be our cue to go to the hospital." I feel his arms scoop me up again, only this time I put up a bit of resistance. "'Nuff of that," he says, tightening his grip. "I'll not add falling down to the list of injuries. Art!" I feel him call over his shoulder (and now mine), "Grab her shoes and my coat and go start my car."

"I didn't see you there. Really. Sorry," comes Art's slightly panicked voice a few seconds later as I am being lugged toward the parking lot.

"Oh, that's not the half of it, Sumners," William Grey growls. "I'll think of ways for you to settle this up later. Right now, Miss Black, watch your head here," his voice strains a bit as he deposits me in the passenger seat of his car. His really nice car I'm about to bleed all over— and maybe worse, given the current state of my spinning stomach.

"I'm…oh…owww. I think my face is broken."

"Lean back against the seat. Put your head here. Hang on to this. There you go." He guides my hand on to the armrest and shuts the door gently before dashing around the car to slip into the driver's seat. He checks me again, gingerly peeling back a corner of the towel. "Well, I think it's not as bad as I first thought."

"I diffagree. Whaf's bleeding? Everything?" I look

at him with one eye, because the other one won't open anymore.

"You've got a nasty gash just above this eye and a scrape here," he points to my left cheek which is slowly swelling into my field of vision. "I don't think you broke your nose. Just bloodied it a bit." He pinches the bridge of his own nose as if in sympathy. "I'm dreadfully sorry. The man's a brute. An idiot. I don't know what to say."

It came over me in an instant. "I want an A for this."

"A what?"

"You're going to gib me an A on my paper for this. I deserbe an A. I'm going to look like a cabe woman with gowilla eyebrowf for a week, or a wacoon with two black eyes, I fink that gets me an A." I stare as hard as I can at him. "Owwww," I add, just for emphasis.

"We don't cover negotiation until week six." He's trying to look stoic, but a laugh percolates behind his eyes.

"Oh really. What week do we cover litigation and liability?"

The laugh escapes. "I'll let you know, but it seems you already know the material." He puts the car in gear, but stops for a moment to dab at my forehead. "Miss Black, I am truly sorry about this."

I'm momentarily astounded by the tenderness in his touch. I didn't expect that. I blink at him for a stunned second, until I notice he has a large blotch of red on the corner of his shirt. "Maggie," I reply, working hard to make the *M* sound like an *M* and not a *B*. "I've bled all over you, you might as well call me Maggie."

"I'm Will," he says. You'd think I'd be in too much pain to notice the indescribable something that changes in his voice and in his eyes. "And the shirt will wash." He pulls out of the parking lot with a cautious turn. "Now let's get you taken care of."

Chapter Six

The art of lumps and gauze

"MAGS!" Diane lets every ounce of her alarm play out in her voice. Who needs a mirror when your best friend gives your new stitches a response like that?

Will guides me to the couch as if the removal of his arm might mean my instantaneous death. Gallant and guilty make a great combination—I haven't been this fawned over since my sixteenth birthday when, instead of going to my party, I had to have my appendix removed.

I lean my head back against the sofa while Will hands off pills, ice bags and other medical goodies to Diane. He's issuing orders, actually; as he places each item in Diane's hands, he spouts off the precise directions I heard earlier from the E.R. doctor. I don't bother telling him Diane's a nurse—this scene is far too amusing and I could really use the distraction. My head feels as though it's been filled with a delightful combination of cement and exploding firecrackers. Diane shoots me a wink while Will puts the four ice bags he bought me at the hospital pharmacy into my freezer. *Four.* Really. Do I look that bad?

All this attention is flattering to a point, but I swear the man's blood pressure has gone up forty percent. He actually yelled at the triage nurse because he thought I wasn't being seen fast enough. Come on—fifty minutes in an urban E.R. is actually rather speedy for your basic nonlethal injury. I attempt assurance. "I'm going to be fine, Will."

"No, you won't," Will replies, looking at me like I'm…like I'm…well, maybe I don't want to finish that sentence. *Disfigured for life* comes to mind. He's peering at me analytically. "If that bleeding starts up again…"

"Diane's a nurse, you know," I confess, because I've decided I hurt too much to be entertained. "I'm in expert hands here. She's going to spend the night and everything." The really strong painkillers they gave me at the hospital are starting to wear off and I want my new prescriptions *now* but don't want to try stuffing a pill into this face with *him* watching.

"You're sure you'll be all right?" he says, sounding doubtful. "You don't need anything?"

I need to change into pajamas, to choke down my pain pills and to curl up in a ball. I can't do that with you watching, your lordship. "Fibe." I say, relapsing into swollen-face speech for his benefit. "I'm tired and I just need sleeb and bills."

"Pardon?"

"Sleep and pills," Diane says, taking his elbow and pulling him toward my kitchen. "She needs to take her medication and sleep everything off. Will, you said your name was, right?"

"William Grey"

The third, my brain adds through the fog.

"Yes, well, the third, but I hardly see how that's relevant at the moment."

Aw, I didn't say that out loud, did I? Pills, where are those pills?

"Okay, William Grey III, give me a phone number where I can call you later tonight and I'll give you a full update once she's had a few hours sleep. You've been a perfect hero this afternoon and I'm sure Maggie will talk to you as soon as she feels up to it."

I sink back into my couch and pull up the afghan my aunt made me. I want to be surrounded by soft, fuzzy things. I want someone to make the aches and pains go away and let me sleep. Face it: even though it's August and I'm twenty-eight, I want to be tucked in under the covers.

I hear Diane usher Will out the door with no less than three more promises to call if my condition should deteriorate in any way.

I shut my eyes until she perches next to me on the couch with a glass of water, a straw, and a handful of pills. "Come on now, time for Maggie to head off to the pain-free place."

She swaps out my ice pack as I down my pills, wincing as she gets another look at me. "Could you stob that?" I mutter.

"You're *sure* you didn't break your nose? They did X-rays?"

"Twice. Will insisted they check again."

"Cute and caring. I'm glad I have his home phone number."

"Diannne…" I growl. "You do *not* get to hit on my loan officer."

Diane sits back. "He's that guy? *That* man was the aloof, stuffy banker who denied your loan? Whoa, maybe you needed a conk on the head. He's gorgeous!"

Near as I can tell, I faded out at around 9:00 p.m. It's just after midnight now and I just woke up, bleary-eyed, sore and very thirsty. Diane somehow got me into pajamas and moved me to my bed, but I don't remember any of that. I grab my bathrobe and stumble out into the living room.

Diane's on the couch, fast asleep, with the TV playing softly on one of those classic movie channels. The screen shows a beat-up boxer getting a you-gotta-get-back-in-there speech from his baseball-capped, gum-chewing manager. One look at our prizefighter reminds me it might be time to brave the bathroom mirror.

I pad toward the kitchen for something to drink. I ignore the three bottles of Gatorade Will brought, opting for a diet soda instead. Gently fizzing bubbles might feel nice. Plus, I can use a straw without feeling like I'm a fourth grader home sick from school.

I catch a glimpse of myself in the microwave window. Wow. I might want to take a few deep breaths—or prayers or maybe another painkiller— before I try anything as accurate as a mirror.

Inhale. Pop the can top. Exhale. Insert straw. Inhale, head toward the bathroom, exhale. Inhale, go into the bathroom, exhale. Inhale, reach for the light switch…

Howl. Yep, that's the word for it. I'm howling.

I look *hideous.* Absolutely hideous. The prize-fighter on TV—blood and all—could beat me in a beauty contest. My cheeks are so puffy I look like I should be gathering acorns for winter. And I haven't even dared to lift the bandages yet. The disturbing colors around those bandage edges are enough to set the room spinning. "Oh…ooo…I'm awwwfuuulll…."

Diane comes stumbling into the room, panicked right out of dead sleep, gasping, "What? Mags! Are you…oh."

"I'm hid-e-ous!" I should have thought more before giving into a good cry. Those tears sting. I half fall, half slump against Diane, who is just awake enough to catch me.

"You're injured, not hideous," she says, yawning.

"I'm purple. I'm lumpy and puffy. You can't even tell where my eyebrows are!" My *S*'s are still slurred by the sheer size of my upper lip. My face is a Technicolor collage of bumps and gauze.

"It's not that bad."

"Are you kidding? Have you looked at me? Even the circus wouldn't hire me."

Diane shoots me a look. "It's not that bad, Mags. In three days you'll just look like you took a nasty hit."

I scowl as best I can. "I *did* take a nasty hit. A really nasty hit. And I was an innocent bystander!"

"Will feels terrible about what happened. The guy called three times and is stopping by tomorrow. I wouldn't be surprised if this apartment has more flowers than a funeral parlor by noon." She looks at me in that conniving way of hers. "Hey, how many guys on a rugby team, anyway?"

"Stop capitalizing on my…my…" I risk another glance in the mirror looking for the right noun. "Awww…" I touch the only part of my face that doesn't look purple—a spot down near my right ear—and cry harder.

Diane grabs my hand and swats the light switch off. "It's clear we should avoid mirrors for at least twenty-four hours. You're due for more ice and medication. And I want you to eat something." Oh, no. She's got her nurse voice on now. All arguing will be pointless—this woman's a professional.

"Okay. I don't know how I'm going to chew, though."

Diane deposits me at my kitchen table and heads toward the fridge. "Already thought of that. I stopped at the market on my way over. Applesauce, yogurt or ice cream?"

I attempt to raise one eyebrow. "What do *you* think?"

"I figured. Coffee ice cream it is. I'll let you off the nutritional hook for six more hours. Come morning, you're back on real food."

"Yes, ma'am."

While she scoops, I attempt to take stock of my present situation. "Let's see. I'm down at least three days of work, since I doubt I'll resemble a member of the human race until Wednesday. I'm down a couple of hundred dollars of medical expenses...."

"Nope."

"What?"

"Will told me he gave the hospital his credit card and told the pharmacy to send all bills to him at the bank."

This bothers me. I'm an adult, with my own credit card and my own health insurance—paltry as it is. I don't need British foreign aid. "I'm injured, not destitute."

"Suit yourself. You're up an A, though."

"Huh?"

"You got an A on your paper and I'm pretty sure Will never even read it."

Diane puts a bowl of coffee ice cream down in front of me with one hand and my class paper with the other. There's a giant red A on the top.

Next to a smear of mud and several drops of blood. I'd laugh if I didn't think it would hurt so much.

Chapter Seven

What rhymes with caffeine?

Lots of things look better in the dawn of a new day.

I am not one of them.

We're putting that aside, thank you, and attempting some form of deportment for my cascade of visitors today. Starting with who else but my parents. Thank goodness for Diane, she held them off for almost a full day. I'm sure that took major negotiations. But they'll be here today to check in on their little darling.

Followed, you can be certain, by a gaggle of brothers and sisters and maybe even a few nephews dying to see if Auntie Mags is as gross-looking as everybody says.

I tried viewing my face as a piece of artwork this morning. I walked calmly into my bathroom, which I've filled with colorful mosaic pieces so that you hardly notice the boring white porcelain tile and fixtures. *See yourself as just another wildly colored mosaic,* I told myself. *Enjoy the riot of color for the energy it brings. Use your artistic side to appreciate the shades of purple and amber, get creative with the application of gauze, explore your interesting profile.*

Well, I didn't really think it would work, either, but it was worth a shot. Color usually cheers me up, but it's hard to find the right lipstick shade to go with contusion. Is it realistic to consider using under-eye concealer on two-thirds of your face? Do drop earrings or studs go better with stitches? When I asked Diane, she threatened to hide my painkillers and make me go cold turkey onto Tylenol. I'm dressed, though, so that ought to count for something. I'm glad it's only August, because it may take months for me to be able to manage a turtleneck sweater over this mess.

I've arranged myself on the couch, attempting a graceful posture, when Diane lets in the parental brigade.

Mom drops her purse on my kitchen counter and makes no attempt to soften her look of utter horror when she sees her precious baby girl. "Margaret Mary Black! Sweet mercy, but you look just awful!"

My dad shoots me a look of serious concern as he settles into his favorite chair at my place, a big, overstuffed wingback I found at a secondhand store on Broadway. The old chair groans under his weight and I get the feeling he'd groan too, if Mom weren't moaning enough already.

"Thanks for reminding me how bad I look, Mom." Guess what? I'm going to spend the whole day watching people's mouths drop open. My own by-invitation-only pity party. Ooo, big fun. "I actually feel better than I look," I offer, not really sure that it's true.

"I should hope so," Mom nearly gasps. She scuttles over to the couch and grabs my hands. "Why didn't you call me right away?"

Because I knew you'd get like this. Because you'd probably be calling around for plastic surgeons when all I really need is painkillers and ice bags. Because I'm twenty-eight, not four. Take your pick. "Diane's a nurse, Mom."

"And I'm your *mother.*" Mom would argue *mother* outranks everyone. The president of the United States could be waiting to award me the Nobel Peace Prize and Mom would still demand to go first. She's inspecting me now, lips pursed, making that infernal *tsk-tsk* noise mothers make. My dad stares at my purple-fringed curtains. He's probably thinking how nicely I match the decor today. "My poor baby," Mom coos, "my poor wounded baby."

I'm trying to crawl toward normalcy here. "Poor baby" is not what I need. I need a cover stick the size of Puget Sound, because I probably *am* as purple as my curtains. I need an adorable hat with a brim that extends clear down to my elbow, and a pair of dark glasses large enough for King Kong. And I could really use a triple-raspberry white-chocolate latte.

Starting with the latte.

I know most coffee junkies are purists, but me, I love all the flavors and toppings we Americans have added into the coffee business. Makes it more like dessert, but with the added bonus of a jolt to your bloodstream. Speaking of jolts, you can mix codeine and caffeine, can't you? I mean, they rhyme and all.

You can imagine my gratitude when, after two hours of family histrionics, Will Grey arrives with precisely that beverage. How'd he know? Who cares. You don't think he noticed that I actually grabbed at the drink with both hands, do you? It only took me three sips to notice that there was a large bouquet of flowers in his other hand. "From Sumners," Will quickly explains, as if it might be unsuitable to even suggest they came from him. "I stood over him myself while he paid for them. I'd have had him come up here, but somehow I wasn't sure you'd welcome the company."

"After my family," I reply, "the Marine Corps would be a respite." I push aside the pile of throw pillows on my brocade couch so there's room for him to sit down. "They're lovely, thanks. Tell Sumners I'll forgive him if he works on his aim."

"That's just the thing," Will says, rubbing his chin. "Art's the best shot on the team."

"I don't think I'll back you up on that one." I feel

the hot coffee work its blissful charm on my bloodstream. After so much ice, the heat feels cleansing. The blend of smooth milk, sharp coffee, silky foam and luxurious flavors—not to mention the vital caffeine factor—revives me. I close my eyes and sigh.

Will picks up a milk-glass vase I had sitting on my coffee table and sets the flowers in it. "I'll give you one thing, Maggie Black, you're in the right business."

"Stopping flying objects with my face?" Hey, I *can* raise one eyebrow (useful sarcasm tool, you know). I couldn't manage that yesterday.

"No, coffee. I've never seen anyone enjoy it quite so much." You know, Will's a much nicer guy than I gave him credit for. There's a natural calm about him. A solidness that I don't think I can put down simply to British understatement. Today, here, he's different. Something in between the suit-clad banker and the mud-spattered rugby player. Reserved, but with a hint of fun peeking through. He sits back down on the couch and I notice how the blue of his eyes changes in different lights. They're more blue than gray this morning. "So," he says gently, "how are you feeling?"

"Swollen. Sore. Like I might want to stay far away from any rugby friends of yours."

Will laughs. "Oh, you should see Art. He's nearly folded over with guilt. It was a laugh, watching such a big lad try to explain it all to the tiny lady at the flower shop. He could barely bring himself to say what he'd done. Enormously funny, until…"

"Until…"

"Until I had him write *Margaret Black* on the card, at which our tiny shop lady turned into a dragon. It seems…"

"You went to GreenThings on Thirty-Sixth, didn't you?" How could I have missed that on the card? No wonder I liked the arrangement so much. "Will, that's where I work."

"Yes, well, I know that. *Now*. Your Mrs…."

"Chang, Nancy Chang. And I'll just bet she let your buddy Art have it." Oh, I would have given anything to see tiny Nancy Chang telling off enormous Art Sumners—in high-velocity Chinese, no doubt. When that woman gets her dander up, you don't even need a translator to know you're in deep, deep trouble.

Will pinches the bridge of his nose again, laughing softly, obviously reliving the scene. "Yes, well I doubt he will recover from his tongue-lashing anytime soon. He was positively beet-red by the time I dragged him out of the store. I was already planning to bring you some coffee, but she nearly marched us around the corner herself. She made Art memorize and recite your favorite drink before she'd let him leave the store.

Now I'm laughing, even though it hurts. "I was wondering how you'd managed to show up with my favorite drink. I don't recall there being a blank for that on those hundreds of bank forms you made me fill out. Thanks for the coffee, by the way," I say, suddenly remembering my manners, "and thanks for the A, too. I was only kidding about that, you know."

"No, you weren't." He counters, his eyes sparkling for a moment before adopting a more professional tone. "And I'll advise you that such a stunt will only work once with me. You'll *earn* every other A you get in my class. And you'll turn in every assignment on time," his voice suddenly softens again, "although I will grant a limited number of injury-related extensions."

I nod, only because I can't figure this guy out. One minute he's my hero, fawning all over me. The next he's a taskmaster, cracking his tutorial whip.

"So," he continues, producing a piece of paper from his pocket and unfolding it on the coffee table for me to read, "I've adapted this week's homework assignment to suit your…limited capabilities."

I attempt to sit up. "My capacities are not limited, they're just under heavy medication right now."

"Three words," Will declares, pointing to the heading on the top of the page. "Your assignment is to identify the three words your ideal customer uses if asked to describe you in ten seconds or less."

There's a tidy little homework sheet, with bullet points and examples and all, complete with three blanks at the bottom of the page for me to fill in my three words.

Three words. I had to fill out twelve forms and now I'm learning about business by coming up with three words?

"That seems a bit simplistic, if you don't mind my saying so."

Will looks like he was expecting that. "Often, the simplest concepts are the hardest to grasp. This exercise gets to the very heart of your brand and the loyalty you want to build in your customers. 'Nail this,' as you would say, and it drives everything else that comes after it."

"Three words. Well, with the surprising bonus of free time I have this weekend, I ought to be able to drum up three words by Wednesday."

Will smiles. He does have a very nice smile. Dignified, but still genuine. Top drawer all the way. "I thought it would suit the circumstances. We'll see you Wednesday, then?" He plants his hands on his knees as if to get up.

"Going so soon?" I blurt out before I can even think. Now where did that come from? Granted, he's far nicer company than a gaggle of hovering siblings, but it's not as though I'm itching to spend time with the guy. I don't even know if he goes to church. I don't know if he takes cream or sugar. I don't know a lot of things about this guy.

So there's no reason for me to be craving conversation with my friendly neighborhood banker. I've gotten more apology than I'll ever need from both him and his gigantic orb-lobbing friend. I need my rest, right?

After a pause that could mean a host of things—from "I've got better things to do on a Saturday than chat with wounded clients" to "actually, I'd really rather not go,"—Will says, "Well, I should be going."

I'm not going to discuss what that pause does to my imagination. I'm not going to discuss anything in my present medicated state. I mean, really, I harbor warm feelings toward *anyone* who brings me coffee.

Chapter Eight

This is America

"Delicious. Satisfying. Friendly. Quality. Intriguing. Addictive. Energizing. Regal. Attentive. *Crud!*"

I'm pacing around my living room, a cup of my best dark roast displayed smack in the center of my coffee table, cataloguing my three words.

Or trying to.

The exercise isn't working. I stop, I sip, I inhale the potent aroma that is a Maggie-brewed cup of java and I picture my ideal customers' response. I see them, hands cradled around the mug, lifting the brew expectantly to their lips in that spectacular moment that is any coffee-lover's first sip of the day. That's the moment I live for. That's the moment my three words should describe. I totally get the purpose of this task.

It's the customer in my imagination that keeps

messing things up. Every time I picture that customer relishing that sip, within minutes that customer becomes Will Grey. How annoying is it that *he* keeps invading my retail daydreams? I shake myself like an athlete, take another long sip and try again.

"Dynamic. Must-have. Blissful. Surprising. Crisp. Multilayered. Guarded…"

Guarded? Who'd ever drink guarded coffee? Nobody wants crisp, multilayered, guarded coffee. It sounds like you're drinking a well-behaved salad, for crying out loud. Will knew how hard this would be. I bet everyone else did this exercise in twelve minutes, but he knew I couldn't just crank something like this out. It's torture, I tell you.

You know, he may even think he's given me a light load. After all, I guess this *is* a simple exercise for business-types. But for an artistic personality, this is asking the world. Now, if I'd had fifteen words to pick, I'd be fine. But narrowing my life's passion down to three words is excruciating. I've been at this for three days and that sheet is still blank. I start back at work tomorrow and if I keep this up I'll be spouting adjectives while I hand customers their floral arrangements. Can you imagine what Nancy will do if I suddenly blurt out *addictive* while handing someone their Boston fern?

By Wednesday at five-forty-five I still hadn't filled in those blanks. I had to be at class in fifteen minutes, I was all dressed, and had almost talked myself into believing the entire world was not staring at my wounded face. Still, I couldn't haul myself out the door.

I tried to convince myself that perhaps it was some sort of post-rugby stress disorder, that I wasn't as recovered from my injuries as I thought. Yeah, I didn't really believe that, either. You and I both know I'm just plain chicken. *Why, Lord?* I gulped out in a desperate prayer. *Why is this so hard? Why am I making such a big deal out of three little words?*

God, in His infinite wisdom, decided that now would be a good moment for an appalling self-revelation. Don't you just hate it when He picks moments like this to dump a bucket-load of unwelcome truth on your head?

It's not the homework assignment.

It's the assigner.

I'm not freaking out at three little words, I'm freaking out at the prospect of seeing Will Grey in the classroom again. At seeing him all suited up and tutorial. I've seen a sliver of the man out of his work mode and I don't know how to deal with him in a purely work setting anymore.

Slow down, Maggie, be careful. You don't know nearly enough about the kind of man Will Grey is to be thinking this way.

Let's try logic. Let's turn Will's assignment on its ear. Imagine, if you will, that God just gave me a sheet of paper and asked me to list the ten qualities I'd want in a guy. *My* ideal customer, as it were. The list would go something like this:

1. Godly
2. Energetic
3. Daring
4. Adventurous
5. Visionary
6. Handsome
7. Artistic
8. Unconventional
9. Romantic
10. Caffeinated

Okay, the last one's not really a priority, but you get my drift. Do you see reserved Will Grey in there anywhere? I don't. I see the *opposite* of Will Grey. Come on, the man's barely caffeinated—and that was the *least* of my priorities.

So why am I still sitting at my kitchen table at 9:30 p.m., staring at an unfinished assignment sheet, eating the last of my coffee ice cream?

That's it. I've got to get out of here. Go take a walk or something. Shake off this weird paralysis that has suddenly taken hold. I grab a sweater, some big sunglasses to cover my injuries—even though it's dusk, stuff twenty dollars into my pocket and head out the door.

I turn the corner and slam, headfirst, into Will Grey. Ouch! Why must every encounter with this man be so painful? "You! Oww. Why does your shoulder have to be right where my forehead is?" I wobble a bit and my glasses fall off.

"Miss Black!" Will gasps, grabbing my shoulder

to catch me. "Oh, you're all right. You are all right, aren't you? You weren't off to find the nearest hospital?" The man's state of alarm looks odd on him. He's usually such an in-control kind of guy.

"I'm…okay…I think." I touch my forehead and blink my eyes a bit. The world spun out of focus for a few seconds and I might have added a new bruise to my already stunning collection, but for the most part I think I'm okay.

Will takes his hand off my shoulder. I hadn't realized it was still there. Okay, I had, but let's not talk about that at the moment. "You weren't in class."

"Uh…yes, I know."

"I was worried something might have happened to you. You should have people checking up on you, you know. Head injuries can develop complications a few days later."

Develop complications? Oh, I think we can safely say we've developed complications. I walked out of the house four minutes ago to escape my problems, not slam headlong into them.

A sudden, terrorizing thought strikes me. "You didn't tell the class what happened, did you? You didn't explain why I wasn't there?"

Will blinks at me. "I *don't know* why you weren't there. Which is why I'm here. But, no, I found it best to leave the telling to you. Or, the not telling. You don't owe your classmates any explanation."

"Oh, good." I say, leaning up against the wall. I'm surprised at how relieved I am to hear that.

"But," says Will, leaning up on the wall beside me, "you do owe *me* an explanation." He crosses his hands over his chest and looks me over. "You're obviously well enough to be up and about. Why weren't you in class?"

Got any ideas how to answer that one? I stall for time. "I just sort of…panicked, I suppose." Then the answer comes to me. "It was that assignment. That's a mean trick to play on someone like me. You can't just boil a life's passion down to three words like that. It's impossible. I've been working on that nasty thing for hours, but the paper's still empty. Not that I don't have words. I've got a list of thirty-seven words taped to my refrigerator. I just can't boil it down to only three."

Will unfolds his arms. "Now do you see what I mean?"

"Okay, fine, you were right. But that's what I pay you for. You're the teacher, it's your job to be right. Right?"

Will shakes his head, as if his proper British brain just doesn't know what to do with me. He freezes, one hand in the air, eyes squinted shut, and you can just see the guy think. Or count to ten to calm down. I'm not sure which until he pops his eyes open and starts to undo his tie. "Have you eaten?"

"If you count ice cream as dinner, yes."

"I was more thinking along the lines of *actual food*."

"Well, then, I suppose no."

"Right then. Let's go get your massive list, and we'll discuss tonight's lesson over a sandwich."

You gotta love the way this guy speaks. American guys would say, "let's go grab a burger," but no, we're "discussing over a sandwich."

I start walking back to my door. "You English and your sandwiches."

"Beg your pardon?"

"You know," I'm laughing as I turn my key in the lock. "Sandwich." I broaden out the *A* in sorry attempt at British. "Cucumber, Earl of, that sort of thing. It's just so funny."

"I hardly see the humor in eating a sandwich." Will follows me up the stairs.

"I know and that's what makes it so funny." I unlock my apartment door, "Hang on, I'll be right back." I snag the list off my fridge, pretend I'm not really checking my hair in the mirror, snag an even bigger pair of sunglasses even though it's dark now and head back to the front door. "List in hand. Let's go have a sandwich."

"Perhaps I should have a hamburger now. Or fried chicken. Something less British." He's got the same expression my brothers have before they launch into a load of teasing.

"Oh, no, I'd like a sandwich." I put on my glasses even though it makes things so dim I have to squint and squinting hurts a bit. I make my way down the stairs, holding the railing tight because I can't really see the stair edge with these glasses on. At the bottom, I turn to find him standing halfway down the stairs, staring. "What?"

"You know, I suggested a sandwich because I *thought* it might be less complicated than going for a coffee."

"Coffee's not complicated." I give him a let's-go gesture and he comes down the last of the stairs to hold the entrance door open for me. Great. It's even darker outside now, so I have even *less* of an excuse to be wearing sunglasses. "Coffee's the most basic thing in the world," I continue, happy to have a safe topic of conversation on which to park my nervous energy. "It's complex, but not complicated. There's a difference. Roasting fine Kenyan coffee beans is complex. You, you're complicated."

"Complicated, am I?" From behind the protection of my enormous shades, I risk a glance at his face. I thought I'd find the glowering teacher who's stared me down in class. That's not who I see at all. I see a surprised, somewhat intrigued man with a disarming glint in his eyes. There's a word for the way he looks, but I can't quite think of it. A spark behind his eyes that makes you want to spar with him because you know it will be so much fun. I should back down, apologize, pretend I meant to say something different, but his demeanor (or is it mine?) just won't let me.

"Highly," I reply, enjoying this.

"Well, one certainly can't resist an explanation for that. Will I be sorry if I ask exactly how it is that I am complicated? Or don't I want to know?"

Come on, there's not a woman on the planet who could resist an open door like that. I place my right hand in front of my face as if spreading out a marquis. "William Grey III. Banker. Three-piece suit. Files with typed labels. A dozen freshly sharpened pencils lined up on his desk. Efficient. Organized. Driven."

Grey looks a little disturbed to know I saw the dozen lined-up pencils, but seems to be enjoying my description.

We turn the corner and I raise my left hand, creating another marquis. "Will Grey. Rugged. Gets dirty for a good cause. Competitive. Heroic. Captain of the guard. Capable, I'm guessing, of very good pranks in school. But never caught."

One look at Grey and I know I've nailed it. I'm good that way. Intuitive. That's important in the coffee business. You've got to know how much cream is too much, how much sugar is not enough. When the woman who says to only put a "smidge" of whipped cream on her latte really means for you to pile it on.

Will chuckles. "Once," he says, looking at me sideways. "I was caught only once."

"And what did little Willy Grey do to get caught at boarding school?"

He raises an eyebrow. "And just how do you know that the incident in question was at boarding school?"

I point to his finger. "The ring. The attitude. Plus, I read enough to know that all proper English lads get into mischief at boarding school. Besides, I imagine after you got caught the first time, you made *very sure* you were never caught again."

Will stares at me. "You're rather frightening, you know. Has anyone ever told you that?"

"My three brothers tell me all the time."

Will's eyes pop. "Three. Brothers. Well, that certainly explains it."

Now it's my turn to stare. "Explains what?"

"You are, without a doubt, the feistiest person I have ever met."

I can't resist. "Will I be sorry to ask why?" I mimic his earlier response. "Or don't I want to know?"

Will grins, pulls open the restaurant door, and says, "Yes, I'm quite sure now coffee would have been less complicated. Even with you."

I don't even want to get into what happened in the pit of my stomach when he said *you*. Let's just say it was *complex*. Determined to keep off that particular subject, I redirect the conversation. "We're not talking about me, we're talking about what you did in boarding school."

"No, I was talking about you and why you missed class. You steered the conversation away from that subject and onto the topic of my childhood misadventures." Will points toward an open booth near the window. "And don't think you'll get away with it. I'll be happy to recount the terrible fate of Madam Fraser's liberated rabbits *after* we've covered the topic of Maggie Black's ideal customer impression."

A spindly, underfed college student sulks over and plants a pair of menus onto the table. Unable to read anything in these glasses, I pull them off and begin looking for the dessert page. He's about to launch into his rendition of today's specials when he gets a clear look at my face. My face, which I've forgotten I've just unveiled. "Whoa, lady, duck next time, okay? Man, what hit you?" he says, cringing right down to his snake tattoo and rock concert T-shirt.

All right people:

1) I'm too young to be called "lady" by college students.
2) Reminders of my current appearance are unwanted.
3) It was entirely unnecessary for his lordship to butt in and growl, "That's clearly none of your concern" in such an intimidating high-and-mighty accent that our server backs away without so much as pouring us a cup of coffee.

I slam my hands onto my hips. "I can take care of myself, you know."

"What an appalling thing to say. He's supposed to be serving you, not insulting you."

Did he hear me at all? Testosterone-based hearing loss? Hello? "And who said you're supposed to be protecting me? I could have handled Mr. Tactful just fine on my own. You just said yourself how feisty I am." I put my sunglasses back on.

"I'm not being protective. He was rude. You

could have been an army general and I would have responded the same way."

I don't believe that for a minute. "You would not," I counter in my best little-sister-fights-back tone. Suddenly all the overblown fussing I've received in the past week boils up inside my independent head. "You're coddling me because I'm a girl. Because I got *this*," I say, pointing to my face, "turning in one of your assignments and because… because…because you've got all that genteel British stuff running around in your veins and you can't help it. And it's annoying. Got it? Annoying. This is America, where women kick butt on a regular basis and the guys can handle it."

The power banker comes roaring out of his features. He jabs a finger at the server "You," he commands, snapping the server to attention. "Coffee, black, two sugars," He says pointing to my place setting. "Tea, with milk and one sugar, very hot," he says, pointing to himself. "You," he says, glaring at me so hard I gulp, "have thirty seconds to take those ludicrous glasses off and narrow your list down to ten words starting *now*."

"You can't…"

"Twenty-eight, twenty-seven…"

Unfair, obnoxious, boorish, egotistical…

Chapter Nine

Two scarier thoughts

"He didn't!"

I'm sitting in my sister Cathy's kitchen after work Monday, looking at photos of Charlie in his toad costume and relating the events of my sandwich with Will. "He did. I swear I thought he was going to whip out a sword and defend my honor or something."

"Guys like that still exist?"

"I know. You'd think the male species would have left the I-must-protect-the-fairer-sex mind-set behind a couple of decades ago. I told him this is America, where the women can hold their own, thank you very…"

I stop mid-sentence because of the look on Cathy's face. She's not sharing my distaste for Will Grey's overprotective tendencies. Rather, she has that dreamy-eyed fairy-tale look she usually gets when talking about her husband. "No. No, Cathy, it's not a good thing. You're not hearing me. I don't like what he did." I over-enunciate the last sentence because she doesn't seem to be registering my meaning.

"Well, it was a bit over the top. It's not like the waiter called you a hag or anything."

"My point exactly. If a thug with a knife comes up to me demanding my jewelry, then I don't mind a little protection from someone bigger than me. But a tactless waiter? Please. I don't need anyone coming to my rescue over bad manners."

"Oh, yes, we all know all about how Maggie Bootstraps gets by just fine on her own."

I hate it when she calls me that. Dad calls me that when he wants to get all fatherly on me, when he doesn't like the way I do something and he thinks he should come in and save the day and I won't let him. Something about pulling myself up by my own bootstraps. Which, by the way, is a good thing. Independence is a good thing. The kind of concept strong enough, say, to found a country on. The United States, for example. No monarchs allowed here, mister, we value the self-sufficiency of every hardworking American. Opportunity. Enterprise. So stop trying to protect me and just give me my loan!

Cathy touches my forehead, conducting a maternal assessment. "Speaking of doing fine, did you have Diane check that out? You didn't need more stitches or anything?" Her eyebrows furrow together as she stares at my remaining collection of bandages and Steri-Strips.

If I had a dollar for every time I've heard that question this week, I wouldn't need a small-business loan. "Yes," I moan, "I'm fine. Will had them X-ray me twice, even, just to be sure.

"Sounds like a nice guy, this Will." She smiles as she rearranges the photos on the table. "And you said he asked you to say grace over dinner? Sounds really nice."

"Don't."

"Don't what?"

"Don't do that. I've had enough of it from Diane. He's…" I stumble, realizing I can't tell Cathy who he is. I'm not ready to tell my family I've gone out in search of a loan to open a business. Oh, great, Cathy's taking my pause as a sign of hidden emotion. Like Will's some kind of secret crush. "Look, I take a class with him, that's all. We were working on a paper together and I was bringing it to him when I got hit. He's just being nice because he's totally guilty."

"Yep," she says, looking like she didn't believe a word I just said. "Whatever you say."

"Don't do that!" *Lord, could I have a different family please? Just for the next seven weeks? There are four other kids—no one would even miss me.*

"Fine. Change of subject. Are you coming to the mission potluck Wednesday? Charlie's choir is singing."

"Can't," I say, happy for the first time in months to

have a reason to miss a family outing. "I've got a class."

"What kind of class is this, anyway?"

I am not ready to talk about this. Even with Cathy. She may be the first to know when the time is right, but that's not now. "A class." I reply, imbuing the words with all the and-we're-not-going-to-talk-about-it tone I can muster. "I've got to get going—it's Diane and my night at the Closet." Every other Monday Diane and I volunteer at the church's clothing ministry, sorting used clothing to give to families who have hit hard times. It's a great deal: we catch up and do good at the same time. "Tell Charlie I think he was adorable and he can be the toad in my pond any day."

As quickly as family courtesy will allow, I gather up my stuff and head for the door. As she's letting me out, Cathy drops the all-too-intuitive-big-sister bomb. "Mags," she says, catching my elbow.

"Yes?"

"Don't pretend you hate it so much. It's nice having someone watch over you."

I gape at her for a stunned moment, mumble goodbye and take her front stairs at a run.

I hate big families. Too many people who are way too familiar with you.

Later that night, Diane stares at me over a large purple sweatshirt. "You really told him off like that? Was that a smart idea? Given who he is and all?"

I tie a pair of knee socks together in a vigorous

knot. "I don't know what came over me. Suddenly, I was so…I don't know, agitated…that it just sort of jumped out of me. I hate it when people coddle me. He was just the last straw of coddling in a very suffocating week. I apologized…twice…but I don't know."

"Well, mouthing off at your loan officer sounds like good business practice to me. And really, I just *hate* it when a man gets honorable and defends you. The *nerve.*"

I launch into a full five seconds of "You got it sister," before I realize she is being totally sarcastic. I stare her down. "Fine, Diane, *you* go after him. People get hurt playing rugby all the time, I'm told. Go watch a game, catch something with your own face and I'm sure you'll have a serious relationship before your wound even scabs over."

"I can't."

Oh, I do not like the way she said that. "And why not?"

"Because *you* like him. And I'm too good a friend for that."

"I do *not.*" Too much emphasis. We both instantly know it to be an outright lie. With one look, Diane reminds me that in the six years I've known her, I've never been able to keep anything from her. It's why she's the only person on the planet who knows my coffee-bar plans.

The only person except for Will, of course. Can I run away now, please? Be a missionary on a shade-grown organic coffee plantation somewhere in the southern hemisphere?

"Well," I relent under Diane's truth-extracting stare. "I can't. Like him, that is."

"And why can't you like him? He's got a list of very likeable qualities."

Of course, if you're Diane, *single* and *male* is as long a list as you need. Let's just say that while Diane is a fine and compassionate Christian, she's way too fond of the male population. Being as cute as she is just feeds the impulse. Don't get me wrong: Diane's not promiscuous or anything, it's just that she seems to like *every single guy* she meets. *Every* guy. Any *single* guy. You get my drift.

"Oh, for starters, he's my loan officer. He's stuffy and formal and proper. He's rigid and foreign and…"

"And you like him and it's making you nuts." Diane jabs a finger at me, her hair swinging with all that emphatic pointing. "What? You think the phrase *opposites attract* popped out of thin air?"

"It's a bad idea. A whopping bad idea. If I want to get this coffee bar open, he and I can't happen. And that's only one of about sixty reasons I can think of why not to get things started with Will Grey. He could have only asked me to say grace because he read about my Christianity on my loan application. Allowing grace over dinner doesn't make him a man of genuine faith. Why are we even discussing this anyway? It's not worth discussing."

Diane puts a final sweatshirt into a box and closes the lid. "Okay, Maggie, why do you want to open this coffee bar, anyway?"

Start with the easy questions, why don't you? "Because I need to." It's so much more complicated than that, but the words aren't coming. Coffee is one of the world's most powerful catalysts. Conversations happen over coffee. Hospitality happens over coffee. Let's face it: *life* happens over coffee. It's the perfect tool to reach people—especially here. Jesus met people where they were, as they were. I want to show people *that* Jesus. While we can't always show people that Jesus in a church, I believe we can show people that Jesus at Higher Grounds. Think about it: very few people might jump at the question, "Can I talk to you about Jesus?" but almost everyone will say yes to "Can I buy you a cup of coffee and talk?"

My life's passion is to set a warm, welcoming stage for conversations that lead people toward a deeper faith. If that sounds like a mission statement, it is. That's my company mission statement for Higher Grounds, and it fires me up faster than a triple shot of the world's best espresso.

"If you don't do this thing you think God wants you to do, do you think you can't be happy?"

Believe it or not, that about sums it up. "Well, yeah, I suppose that's it. I've been such a noncommittal basket case. I've held a dozen different jobs since college. I liked them all, but I didn't really care about the work. Now, I can't stop thinking about the work, everything up to now feels like it's led up to doing this. I *know* it's what God wants for me."

Diane leans in. "What if what God wants for you is to meet Will? Have you ever considered that Higher Grounds might just be His way of introducing you?"

A scarier thought could not exist. "No, It's not like that. It can't be like that."

"Why?"

I sit down on the stool and hold my head in my hands. Why indeed? "Because Higher Grounds is…is me. It's who I'm supposed to be, what I'm supposed to do. I know that. Finally. I won't ever stop knowing it. And it's nothing at all like who Will is and what Will does. He's in a whole other world over there. A world that doesn't mix with my world over here. I don't want to end up thinking 'What if?' thirty years from now, wondering if I gave up my world to fit into his. I need to reach for this. I watched my dad come home from work at this ordinary job when he wanted to be a sculptor. He dreamed of being a sculptor, not an insurance agent. And he could have—that's the thing. He's so talented. He could have done such amazing things. But he fell in love with Mom and then *boom!*— married with five kids to support." I throw the knee socks into a box and reach for a new pile of clothes to sort. "I know he's happy. He'd tell you he's happy. But…"

"But what?"

"But if he walks past a sculpture garden or if he looks at a statue, you just see it in his eyes. The 'What if?' He settled. Not in a bad way, I suppose, but settled just the same." I look up at Diane. "I just don't think I can do that. Settle. I'd never really be happy."

"What if, instead of settling, you got the best of both worlds? Will's some kind of business expert, right?"

"So he tells us every time he hands out new homework."

"What if Will Grey is just what you need? Personally and professionally?"

I give Diane my best "mind your own business stare" and push a pile of unsorted clothes across the table at her. "I'm telling you, the last thing I need is another personal dose of William Grey in all this Thirdness."

Chapter Ten

Attack of the "Anti"

This is all his fault, I tell you.

Don't think for a second that I had any other choice in the matter. It's his silly assignment that got us into this ridiculous argument and, honestly, I didn't think it'd turn out quite this bad.

Still, some guilty part of me enjoys watching William Grey III squirm though the most frilly, girlie-girl tea service Seattle has to offer. It shouldn't amuse me that his hand can't even fit through the teacup handle. This probably violates the Geneva Convention on the treatment of loan officers. He looks like he's going to tumble off that prissy little chair any minute now.

"Have you a slightly larger cup?" Will's making a heroic effort and getting through this with his dignity intact. The snickering pack of grandmothers to our left aren't helping. And I did wince (if only inwardly) when the lace-covered eight-year-old pointed at Will and asked in a delightfully loud voice "Mommy, why is *he* here? He's a boy!" I planned on taking Will Grey to tea, not taking him down a peg with his own weapon...ahem... beverage of choice.

Okay, okay, I know you want to know how we got here. Believe it or not, it was Will's own class homework. The one he assigned after the infamous three-word list. He told us to come up with a list of things we'd *never* do with our business. Sort of the anti-Higher Grounds. Which, after class, got us into a discussion of whether or not my coffeehouse would serve tea. Which got us into a discussion of the merits of coffee vs. tea. Which, despite our calm and mature adult natures, regressed into an argument about how tea is for sissies (granted, my words, not his). He got under my skin—again. He was making it sound like grunting lowlifes go for coffee and the world's finer intellects understand the complex nature of tea. I can get into an argument with this guy at the drop of a hat.

He told us that we'd get extra points for using vivid descriptions in our assignments. Sign me up for that extra credit, because how much more vivid can you get than to actually take the teacher there? I looked for the highest high tea I could find a booked and table for two. Who knew I would find the fluffiest, stuffiest, girliest, lace-and-doily-coated high tea in town?

So, it's not completely my fault that he's sitting in a tiny chair, surrounded by chintz and ruffles, attempting to get his large hand around a teacup the size of a plum. His knees barely fit under the table. Still, it meets the assignment: there's nothing fun or funky or hip about this place. There's potpourri oozing out of every crevice. Harp music lilts out of a corner filled with stuffed cats and baby dolls. We're surrounded by violets and baby's breath. This is everything I don't want Higher Grounds to be. In dainty stereo sensaround. It looks like we stumbled into a nineteenth-century girl's dollhouse.

I'm not even sure the tea they serve here qualifies as caffeine. I can still see the china pattern at the bottom of my cup and I've let this brew steep for twice the normal time.

I was just starting to feel really guilty when the waitress started staring at him. Ogling, actually. It only took three words of his British accent to start the wait staff falling over him as though he were some kind of celebrity.

"Would this do?" A waitress appears with—and I don't know how they pulled this off—a masculine teacup. Not quite a mug, but a hefty cup with a hefty saucer. *Hey, if I have to endure this itty-bitty cup for my faint brown liquid, everybody does!*

"Splendid!" he says, sounding like the king of England. Our waitress coos. "And might you have anything along the lines of roast beef? Something with meat in it."

"Oh," she says, "we've just the thing." With a giggle, she darts off behind the kitchen curtains.

"Roast beef is not part of high tea," I point out, trying to keep an upper hand on the situation. "We're supposed to be having high tea. We're on assignment."

"I cannot believe I let you goad me into this," Will says, taking great care to unfold one leg without knocking over the entire table. "Every ounce of testosterone in my body is working in overdrive to maintain the manly dignity currently under fire in my present surroundings."

I'm pretty sure I've just been chastised.

Those steely eyes pin me to my chintz. "Not to put too fine a point on it, Miss Black, but men drink tea. Men *enjoy* tea. In the orient, men spend years studying and mastering the art of tea. I drink tea. I *like* tea. I do not like coffee. And no matter how many tiny cucumber sandwiches you subject me to, no matter how much lace you surround me with, I am a man—an Englishman. I drink tea. I'm fine with that. And those facts *will not change.*" His smile is gleaming and victorious. "Although, I'd have suggested a far less flattering frock if you were looking to do me in." He takes a bite, "mmm"ing in such a way that our waitress erupts in more blushing giggles. "Against all odds, I find myself rather enjoying the afternoon."

Flattering frock? Frock? Did he just compliment my dress?

I have to give this guy serious credit. Any one of

my brothers would be frying like an ant under a magnifying glass if this happened to them. And he's "rather enjoying the afternoon."

I have underestimated my opponent. It is battle we're in, isn't it?

"I'd be remiss if I didn't extend an invitation in return, wouldn't I?" Will says, taking another bite. How did he gain control of the conversation like that? "You do own a pair of trainers, don't you?" He pulls out a pen and begins to write something down on the back of a business card.

"A what?"

"Trainers." He squints in thought for a moment. "Athletic shoes. Sneakers, I believe you call them?"

"Um, yes."

"Splendid. And you're free tomorrow afternoon around three?"

"I get off work at two."

Never, never underestimate your banker.

Or take him to tea.

"Oh, no."

"No, really, Maggie, I think this is definitely what you need."

I am suddenly aware of the near-foot Will Grey has over me. I'm not short, but he's tall. They're all tall. All of them have Will's height, but most of them are twice as heavy. I'm standing in a patch of grass staring at a line of enormous men. Human fortresses in striped shirts. "No sirree, what I need is to stay clear of rugby fields for the rest of my life."

"Pitch, actually. Rugby *pitch*. And conversely, I think getting on a rugby pitch is exactly what you need. Back on the horse that threw you, as it were."

"There will be no throwing of anything in my presence. Show a little mercy here, the bruises are finally fading."

"Yeah," says a man I instantly recognize as my assailant, Arthur Sumners. "Really sorry about that. And so," Arthur grins, "show 'er, boys."

With that the line of men steps aside to reveal a bench with six rugby balls on it. Each taped down—repeatedly—with multiple strips of duct tape. Half of them are snickering, the other half are staring at Will, who merely salutes me. "Precautionary measures," he states. "You're the *only one* allowed to hold the ball today."

Should I be flattered? Or frightened?

"Now," says Will, not quite keeping the laugh out of his voice, "This is a rugby pitch. It's about the size of your football fields. Like football, you try to score points by getting your ball across the goal line, only we call it a 'try' instead of a touchdown. Any of those three brothers teach you to throw?"

"Yes," I reply, slowly and suspiciously, not liking at all where this is going. I believe I'm being subjected to the anti-high tea here. Will goes on about fly-somethings, backward throws (they throw backward?) and I've no idea what a scrum or a line out is, although he told me. What I did hear was the word *tackling*.

There will be no tackling.

I heard the word *maul* somewhere in that description, too, and it didn't do much for my sense of calm.

"Sorry I could only get half the team here, but I think you'll get a feel for the game anyway." Will says after introducing each of the giants by name.

That's only half of them?

"Ready?"

"No!"

"Brilliant. Now take the ball…"

When it is all over, Will points a muddy finger at me. "Admit it. You had fun."

"I'm filthy."

He picks up the sack of equipment and hoists it over one shoulder. "But unharmed. And you had fun."

I adopt a poor mimic of Will's accent. "Despite all odds, I found myself rather enjoying the afternoon."

Will laughs. I feel the sound in the pit of my stomach. He is muddier than I—which is saying something—and his hair hangs down playfully in his eyes. His chin boasts a reckless smudge of dirt. "You did." After a moment, he adds with a quiet grin, "I did, too."

Did I have fun? I had a wonderful time. I saw an energetic, lighthearted side of William Grey that tugged at me in ways I didn't expect.

I want to know more about this man. His past, what he thinks about God. About his politics and what his favorite music is. Where he got that scar above his right eye and what his family thinks of

him being so far from home. I find myself asking
God to let me know he's a man of faith, because my
attraction to him is growing faster than I can handle
if he isn't.

Before I can stop myself, I reach out and pull a leaf
from his hair. Our eyes lock, frozen by the moment.

"Maggie," he says after what feels like an hour,
his expression undecipherable.

"Mmm, hmm," I'm too stunned to attempt an
actual word.

"I find you—" he shifts the bag on his shoulder
and shuffles a foot in the grass "—far more appealing than I should, given our situation."

What does a girl say to that?

"I shouldn't even be seeing you outside of
class, but…" he doesn't finish the sentence. He
doesn't need to.

He feels it, just as I do. I'm suddenly dizzy and
my stomach just left the county. "Will…"

"This is dangerous. Maggie, the consequences of
this are enormous. For both of us. Whatever is…
happening…between us…well…it's not a very
good idea. You see that, don't you?"

"Yes," I reply far too quickly, spooked by the fact
that he feels this spark between us. "I mean, of
course I see that. And there really is…nothing…
happening…" my voice just trails off because that's
ridiculous, we both know there is something happening. A very big, very scary something neither of
us invited.

"It's not just the business side of things,

Maggie." Will lets the bag of gear slide off his shoulders and looks straight into my eyes. Oh, those eyes. They could pull you right inside them if you weren't careful. "We are both people of faith. I know we haven't discussed it, but it is the case and it means that we need to be careful." He shifts his weight and continues, "I hope it doesn't surprise you that I take my faith as seriously as you do. We shouldn't be casual about this. Not that I don't…" He pushes out a breath. "I'm speaking in rubbish here. What I'm trying to say is that…I think we need to be very cautious about how we spend any time with each other outside of class."

Will Grey is a man of faith. Genuine, deep faith.

He's my banker. He's my teacher. Oh, Lord, how could You? How could You send someone into my life who's so right and so wrong all at once?

Chapter Eleven

Is God in the details?

Will Grey draws a neat, perfect square on the whiteboard. "Square footage. For those of you in the retail sector, this is the measuring stick for ninety percent of your operations. For those of you in the service sector, it's less important depending on the type of business you're proposing, but it can't be overlooked." He's in a dark suit and tie tonight, one-hundred-percent serious businessman. I wonder if it's for my benefit.

"Josh Mason." Will points at the man I call cyber-guy. Josh wants to fire up VibeNet, the next fabulous people-connecting Internet engine. Long hair, knit cap, artful glasses, goatee. Handsome and charismatic but with a geeky edge. A haircut that looks like he never combs it but probably ran him two hundred dollars. Drives to class in either a Jeep or one of those European scooters. His laptop is hands-down the coolest gadget I've ever seen. And you should see his cell phone. I have a feeling I'll be seeing Josh on the cover of *Small Business Tycoons Monthly* in five years, if not fewer.

"Yep?" Josh pokes his head up over his laptop.

Believe it or not, Josh is my ideal Higher Grounds customer. Think about it: how likely is someone like Josh—in all his intellectual superiority—to darken the door of a church? I know this is a sweeping generalization, but it will be the same type of sweeping generalization that will keep Josh from ever giving Christianity a serious thought. You've got to fight that kind of thinking out in the everyday grind of the real world, not from a church pew.

I could get Josh to show up at Higher Grounds for a cup of coffee. He might resist at first, but I'd get him eventually. Then, we'd start doing what people do over coffee—talk. And even though I could never match philosophical wits with Josh, I could introduce him—over coffee, of course—to someone who could. A lively, engaging debate would ensue. That's where things would get interesting. Where Josh meets people who think like him, but have discovered that Jesus makes sense to people who think like him.

All this happens because we've found a common ground for people of faith to meet people who need faith. An accessible meeting place where faith meets the world and the world meets faith. Where *common ground* gets taken to a *higher ground*.

Ahem. I've digressed just a bit. But now you see my passion for the subject. You see why I can't let this dream go no matter how high the price.

Back to today's lesson.

"Josh, what kind of square footage do you need?" Will asks.

"I'm in cyberspace, man." Josh spreads his hands. "No walls, no limits."

"Just you, your brilliance and few gigabytes, that's it?"

Josh smiles confidently. "That's the beauty of it. Tiny start-up cost, millions to be made."

"Planning to explode on the scene, work like a dog for two or three years, then sell it for a multi-million-dollar profit and retire to Fiji, are you?" Will sits on his desk. I've noticed he always sits like that before making a big point.

"Something like that, yeah."

"And the computers, electricity, files, paperwork, desks, lamps and such go where?"

"Got that all figured out," replies Josh. "I got a huge garage with a heater in it. Half of Silicon Valley started in a garage, so I figure I'm just keeping with tradition."

"And when VibeNet goes global," Will gets up and returns to the whiteboard, "which, of course, it will, you'll need employees and their files and their computers and their desks and—" he throws a look over his shoulder to the class "—is there anyone here waiting for their chance to work in a garage?"

"I'll have my millions by then so it won't be a problem."

"There's where you're wrong." Will draws a long line from one end of the whiteboard to the other. He makes a big dot at the left end and writes Launch above it. "I'm not saying you won't make millions, Josh, but you can't *assume* you'll make millions." He makes a mark two-thirds of the way down the line. "It'll take you six months to find an adequate facility that can grow as fast as your company can."

Will draws a squiggly line back from the two-thirds mark to a new mark one-third down the line. "You'll need to know exactly when you're six months out from expansion, what benchmarks you'll hit when you get to that stage and how much extra capital you'll need to make it happen." He puts a question mark over the one-third mark he just drew. "In short—and this lesson is for all of you—you can't just make it up as you go along. Business is too unforgiving for that." Will stares right at me. "For someone like Maggie, with very high start-up costs and high customer variables, it's absolutely crucial. Your plan, Maggie, may be the most crucial of all."

He's never called me Maggie in front of the class before. And he's singling me out. As someone who needs the most help. I think I'm entitled to get my dander up in this circumstance. Why couldn't he go pick on Mr. Mushroom Pasta Sauce over there? He's got to buy a whole industrial kitchen and packing facility. That's got to be more complicated than a coffee shop.

So now you understand why I stomped down the

hallway after Will the minute class was over. "What's the deal singling me out?"

"Maggie, I…"

"And you called me Maggie in class. Forget the Miss Black? All of a sudden it's Maggie?"

Will thumps his stack of books down on his office desk. "Very well then, *Miss Black,* I'll be more careful in the future." His eyes darkened over in a split second.

"Fine."

"And I did not single you out."

"You did. Jerry Davis has the same issues as me. If not more. I didn't see you pointing at him."

"I did not point at you. And Jerry Davis has already turned in a comprehensive financial plan. With his *first* loan application. Unlike you."

That was a low blow. "So what on earth is he doing in class?"

"Because he needs to learn marketing and salesmanship. *Unlike you.*"

Earl Grey must have been captain of the debate team. He just put me in my place and complimented me at the same time. That's not fair. "I hate that planning stuff. I'm terrible at it. Most of it seems useless to me when you factor in all the stuff than can affect a business like mine."

Will simply glares. He could silence a pack of my nephews with a single glance.

"I hate this stuff," I repeat. "I think you know I hate it. It takes all the faith out it."

Will looks both surprised and exasperated. Like

he thinks I'm blaming him—which, of course, I sort of am. "This is business," he says, his glare softening into something more like concern. "This has nothing to do with faith."

"You're wrong." In fact, he couldn't be more wrong.

"Am I?"

Okay, I wasn't going to get into this with him, but he's asking for it. "You read my application. You know this is a coffeehouse with a Christian atmosphere. It has everything to do with faith. You told me on the rugby pitch that you're a man of faith. You, of all people, should respect the fact that God gave me the vision to open this coffeehouse. I've not been able to think about anything else since He gave me this idea. This is God's plan and I trust Him with the rest of it. Trust, Will. Surely you get that. Trust and faith, even in business. Maybe especially in business. What I'm doing is all about faith and business. Because for me—and lots of other people God took very seriously—business is all about faith. Did Joseph have a business plan to become Pharaoh's right-hand man? Did Moses have an itinerary before he left Egypt? God doesn't always give us the plan. That's why it's *called* faith."

Will looks momentarily blindsided by my speech. I cross my arms over my chest to keep myself from saying *So there!* at the end of my lesson on Faith Without Facts.

"You're wrong."

How can he state it so simply like that? I'm

revising my three-word list on Will Grey. *Exasperating* now tops the list.

"I am not." *Ooo, clever comeback, Mags.* Please. That's the second time we've had that little juvenile exchange. What is it about this guy that gets me into argue-mode so quickly?

Will holds up a single finger. "Joseph," he replies, glaring me down, "had a long-range plan that covered fourteen years of feast and famine." He ticks off another finger. "Moses gave specific directions to divide the people up into tribes so that they traveled in distinct groups with distinct responsibilities. Which makes him," he folds his fingers into a point aimed straight between my eyes, "the first biblical occurrence of management delegation, if you care to know. And even Noah had specific building plans, down to the square cubit, mind you. Square footage, Miss Black. Just like we covered in class. Faith and planning are not enemies."

"Fine. Facts are good. Check. But don't you see? I don't need to know all the details now. What I need is to get *started* now."

"Don't you see?" Will fires back. "You *are* getting started. This is part of getting started. It doesn't all begin the moment you fill someone's coffee cup and take their money." His look is so intense that my throat tightens. "You have passion. You have vision. You live for what you're going to be doing. All those things are vital and they'll take you far. But they'll only take you *so* far." Will takes a breath, as if catching himself up. "Look at it this way," he continues in a softer voice, "it takes a while to get the details lined up, but the faith is knowing *you will get there.*"

"Do you believe I'll get there?" I blurt out, suddenly consumed with the need to know his answer.

"I believe part of God's plan for Higher Grounds is that you get your tactics straight before you get there. And I believe," he continues even more quietly, "that you are here because God wants you here. And I am here because God wants me here."

There is a stunned powerful silence between us. Something hugely important was just said.

"And I believe," Will says with warmth stealing back into his voice, "that those things are not in opposition to each other."

Well, folks, there you have it: the world's first declaration of mutual faith and begrudging admiration conducted by argument. Are we visionaries or what? I lean against his office doorway. "How come we're so good at this?"

"Good at what?"

"Arguing."

"I could say because I'm always right and you're always wrong—"

"Hey!"

Will makes a surrender gesture, both hands flying up into the air. "—but that would only start another argument, wouldn't it?" He smiles and the air between us is filled with something warm and energetic and…highly dangerous. We linger in it for a moment—too long a moment—until Will clears his throat and reaches for another book. "Yes, well, you'd best be going."

"Yes, of course. Lots to do." I gather up my stuff. As I head out the door, he calls out.

"Miss Black?"

"Yes?" I turn, expectant for no reason at all.

"Keep the faith, Maggie. I'll get you there."

Chapter Twelve

A whole lot more bearable

"No, Margaret, don't."

Nancy Chang nearly drops her floral sheers, her eyebrows lowering ominously as she prepares to launch into one of her speeches. Only I'm not in trouble now—well, not really. I've just told her I'm leaving GreenThings to work for a large coffee-bar chain for three months. No, the other one: Carter's Coffees. Seattle used to be the only city where that would be a multiple choice question. The rest of the world is catching up rapidly, however. And I'm going to work for the establishment. For Carter's Coffees, the big bad guys the whole world thinks is out to get all the little coffee shacks, booths, kiosks and independent shops that can be found on nearly every corner of this city.

You'd think I just told her I was going to work

for some sort of orphan-beating gangsters. Her reaction was that strong—and that negative. And that was just the part of the speech that was in English. When Nancy really gets riled about something, she switches to Chinese, even though she speaks perfectly good English. Carter's Coffees got called a few choice names in Chinese. I didn't ask for a translation.

I told Nancy I might be coming back afterward—but only because she looked like she might crumble into tiny bits.

But I'm not coming back. Those three months are just an education. On-the-job training. Every article and every book I've read on how to open your own coffee bar suggests you do a stint at one of the big chains to learn the ropes. At first, I admit I thought it way beneath me. I don't like those guys, even if their consistency has won them international acclaim. But you have to admit, they might know their stuff. Anyone making upwards of four dollars on an infusion of tiny brown beans people used to only pay thirty-five cents a cup for can't be that dumb.

I didn't see that until Will explained the value of research. The widespread error of entrepreneurs reinventing the wheel. Then, I saw the brilliance in it. Why repeat someone else's mistakes? Take brand X's hideous layout and change it while you employ brand Y's excellent brewing consistency. Visiting them is one thing—and trust me, I've visited them all hundreds of times. But working there, I'll see their dark underbelly. It's a great strategy, provided I can stomach the oh-so-trendy souls some of these stores pull in as employees. Come on, you know what I mean. Those activist-rock-star types who sneer at you for insisting on whole milk instead of the organic gluten-free shade-grown soy they'd recommend.

I'll just think of it as a mission field. That's right, I'm on a mission from God and I will not be shaken.

Except, maybe, by the icy look in Nancy Chang's formidable eyes. "You are so much better than that!" she pronounces in her clipped accent. "Wait-ress." It sounds like a curse the way she says it.

"Barista," I correct her.

She shoots me one of her looks. Why do I attract people with death-ray eyes into my life?

"That big place? With no heart or soul? Did I teach you *nothing?*" She makes an indignant noise through her nose, looking at me as if I'm about to take the express train to my own doom. "You'll be back."

As far as she's concerned, any company with more than fifty employees is corrupt and can't be trusted. They don't call my neighborhood The Artists' Republic of Fremont for nothing.

"You know how much I love coffee," I offer, collecting fern leaves into a plastic bin. A burst of highly dramatic music from the tiny black-and-white television playing her Chinese soap opera seems to punctuate the moment. "I'll be happy," I declare, just because I need something to say or I'll squirm right out of my skin. When it fails to placate,

I retreat into the storage refrigerator, putting away the ferns and escaping her ongoing glare.

"You'll hate it by the end of the month." She calls, clipping a leaf stem with a nasty *snip*.

"Come on now, Nancy, do you hate flowers just because you work with them every day?" I ask, coming out of the refrigerator. "Sure, it's corporate coffee, but it's still coffee. *I* drink their stuff."

Nancy selects a bird of paradise and inserts it into the arrangement she's creating. Her words are as spiky as the bloom. "I am not a machine for making money." She adjusts the bloom until it is angled just so, turning the vase this way and that to check the lines. "I am an artist making beauty. I make beauty every day." She stops, satisfied with her design, then points the shears at me and growls, "You, you will just be making coffee for grumpy, tired people who couldn't care less."

For all her angry judgment, Nancy's got a point. A good segment of your coffee-bar-customer population is grumpy and tired. Lots of people go to coffeehouses for celebration and conversation, but there's a whole other sector that just want their caffeine fix. The faster, the stronger, the better. If chatting them up while I get the milk temperature j-u-s-t right takes ninety seconds more, they might go elsewhere. Someplace with a drive-through. Something, by the way, that I don't want.)

My customers will walk in. And they'll walk in again and again after they taste my triple-shot caramel macchiato. My brother called it my

Porsche Potion because it was smooth and super-powered like the sports car.

That's me. Zero to sixty in under ten ounces.

"From order to drink in under six minutes."

That's lesson number one at Carter's Coffeeschool. I'm sitting in yet another stark classroom, crammed into one of those desk-chair contraptions I remember from high school. How did I go from a great life to not one but *two* kinds of classes each week?

Coffeeschool isn't coffee, it's math. Formulas. Slogans and acronyms. Step by step preparation outlines. Manuals. Forms to fill out. *Forms,* for crying out loud. You remember how much I hate forms, right?

Remind me why doing a stint at corporate was a good idea last week? Remind me why I'm dragging myself through the rain and traffic downtown every day instead of walking three lovely, art-filled blocks to work amongst the blossoms?

"I hate forms," says a deep voice with a Latin-American accent to my left. I look up to see a pair of espresso-brown eyes peering at me from over an employee manual. "Nobody ever brewed a great cup of coffee using a spreadsheet."

"As a filter, maybe?" I reply, thinking I may have found a kindred free spirit amongst the corporate rank-and-grounds.

"Think they'd let us? I'd start with page 134." My conspirator is a friendly young man about my age with long, wavy brown hair. He wears an olive green T-shirt and tan cargo pants. Sort of an exotic adventurer look that not every guy could pull off—not that successfully, anyway. "That whole chapter is useless," he continues. "But then, what kind of brew would come out of boiling water and laser-printer ink?" He mimes tearing the page out of the manual. "Not organic in the slightest." He smirks a bit at the thought, then extends a hand. "Renato Oliviera." He has the coolest ring I've ever seen. "But everyone usually calls me Nate."

"Maggie Black."

"Glad to meet you, Maggie Black. What number?"

No, he's not asking for my phone number, he's asking for my store number. We all were hired by different stores across the city, but we spend our first three days in training here at—and I will try not to choke on this phrase—corporate headquarters.

"Twenty-six." In Belltown. Not as bad as the heart of the financial district, but not my beloved Fremont, either.

"Hey, me, too." And how did I miss the even cooler cross around his neck?

"I'm thinking store number twenty-six just got a whole lot more bearable," Nate says with a grin.

You know, I was just thinking the same thing.

Carter's Coffees—store number twenty-six—*was* a treasure trove of information. For example, your average coffee-bar employee stays on the job about eight seconds. No, not really, it's more like 1.5 years, but it feels like eight seconds. Turnover is a big issue in this business. You've just gotten someone trained and they go off to law school or Microwhatever to get their real job.

Nate Oliveira and I became better friends as the week went on. Very cool guy. Artistic spirit, friendly, witty, loves coffee and—drum roll, please—committed Christian. Kindred spirit indeed! *Thanks, God.*

I mastered store number twenty-six in the first four hours. I admit it, the bank's business classes are giving me an advantage here. I grasp the bigger picture better than most of the new employees (and lots of the old employees, for that matter). I'm feeling supersmart and my manager treats me very well. Should I be impressed with myself that I was managing a shift in my first week? Or unimpressed with Carter's standard for management material?

In any case, when the time came to do my equipment worksheet for class, I had it all right here in the manual. I used their list as a template, upgraded in a few places, lost the boring tableware and the nasty logo aprons, and turned in my assignment *early.* Early! Even Will's secretary, Bea, had her mouth open at that one. She gave me three peppermints out of her jar and a very approving look.

Why the promptness, you ask? Because the big bad brewing corporation wouldn't give me Wednesday night off no matter what I said. My beloved auntie could have been on her deathbed, gasping to bequeath her millions to me with her final breaths, but unless I'd already accrued two hundred work hours, I'd still be stuck slinging coffee.

So I missed class.

After I've missed enough class already.

I suppose, then, that I shouldn't have been surprised when his lordship showed up at good ole store number twenty-six at the end of my shift. Looking supremely British and supremely agitated.

"You *are* here. Brilliant."

I wiped the surprise off my face while wiping down a table. "No kidding. Why so stunned?"

Will swipes a hand down his face and looks around. "Well, when Bea handed me your assignment and your note, I'm ashamed to say I didn't believe her."

Points for honesty. No points for tact. "You thought I was cutting class?" Of course, right after I said that, I realized he had *every reason* to think I was cutting class. I cut class before for pure vanity. Cutting for something else—*anything* else—should be easy to believe.

"Maggie Black unable to attend class because she's taken a job at Carters? A giant corporate chain coffeehouse?"

"You said it would be a good idea," I counter.

"My point exactly. You don't have a history of agreeing with my good ideas."

Nate comes out from the back room with a box of napkins. "Friend of yours?"

Now, how would you answer that question? I decide not to. "Nate Oliveira, this is William Grey."

Nate extends a hand. It looks odd: artsy Nate shaking hands with suit-clad Will. "Pleased to meet you, Nate," says Will. Nate just nods.

"Come to get Maggie off her shift?"

"Well…"

What do you know? Inscrutable William Grey actually flusters.

Chapter Thirteen

The decent or the messy?

I turn the lock and punch in the store security code while Will practically stands guard over me at the store's back entrance. "I didn't expect you to track me down at work."

"I wanted to make sure you really were here and not...well...not avoiding class because we'd argued last week." Will pinches the bridge of his nose again. I think he's done that six times in the ten minutes it took me to close the store.

"We didn't argue."

He raises that suspicious brow at me.

"Well," I revise, "we sort of discussed. Several topics. Faith and business and how never the twain shall meet or something like that. But I told you where I was going to be."

"And can you see, perhaps, why I was surprised

and not entirely convinced?" Will points to my Carter's apron. I snatch it off, annoyed. "You took my advice."

Do I detect astonishment in his voice? "Not really."

"I suggested it would be a good idea for you to work in a corporate coffeehouse setting for a while before opening up your own shop. You took my advice." Is it really necessary that he look so stunned? Do I come off that uncooperative?

"You and lots of people. Internet guides, books, magazine articles. There was a general concurrence on the subject."

"How is it going?"

I lean back against a tall planter on the corner. The sun is glinting off Elliott Bay nicely tonight and there's no threat of rain. The low-slung clouds reflect an orange glow over the city. A lush, price-less remnant of late summer still determined to hang in the air. "I'm learning a lot," I reply, "about people. Business. How gardeners will come by asking for your grounds and homeless people will come by asking for your leftovers."

"Interesting." Will is tall enough to take a seat on the far end of the same planter I'm leaning on. "What else are you learning?"

"About how a profitable store should pull 300 drinks per shift during peak periods. That sixty percent of people will add a baked good to their order if you suggest it. How was class?"

"You know," Will says, crossing his arms, "it

seems our conversation factor goes down by a good fifty percent without your presence."

"I am sort of mouthy in class. Sorry about that."

A smile sneaks across his face. "I haven't yet decided if it's a bad thing. Class wasn't nearly as interesting without the discussions you tend to stir up."

Now I'm smiling. I didn't see the flecks of auburn in his hair before now. Is there something on my shirt? He's staring at me. My hair must look like it's on fire in this light. That's bad, right? No one wants to converse with a flame torch.

We stumble into a silence for a moment, both finding the bay a safer place to look. Will clears his throat. I fiddle with my handbag. A car drives by with thumping grunge music blaring out the open windows. "Your assignment was well done," he says when the noise settles down. "And early, even."

"I thought it might be nice to surprise you." I laugh a bit but it comes out all wrong. This is one of those moments where you wish life came with a Control+Z—you know, the undo key combination on your computer.

"I was. Surprised, rather. Not that I didn't think you capable—quite the contrary. I think you made excellent choices in where to invest and where to cut back. Risky but bold decisions. Perhaps I'd rethink one or two but I…" he sputters to a stop. "I can't ever say anything clearly around you."

I hoist myself up to sit on my end of the planter. It's surprisingly warm for an early fall night. Crisp and clear, but still summery enough to lure you outside. The tree in the planter hangs onto the last few of its leaves, its branches casting scattered lines of shadow across the ground. We're about two feet apart, but I'm not sure if it feels like two inches or two miles. I notice little details about him, like the smattering of freckles above his cheekbones. The way his eyes crinkle up when he smiles (or grimaces). His cuff links. When's the last time you saw a guy wearing cuff links? Who wasn't in a rented tux? "How'd you get here?" I ask.

Will brushes the fallen leaves off the planter edge. They tumble around each other as the evening breeze pushes them down the sidewalk. "You told me which store number. I could guess the neighborhoods you'd be willing to work, so a quick Internet search pulled up the store."

I giggle. "I meant how did you end up in Seattle?"

He flushes a bit and his mouth tightens around the edges. Oh, no: wrong question. I can tell in an instant. He doesn't answer right away, but finds more leaves to clean off the planter.

"Look, I'm sorry," I backpedal, "that's probably none of my business."

"No, no," he replies quickly, and I see a flash of something dark behind his eyes. "It's just that I was trying to decide if I should give you the quick, decent answer I give my mom or the far messier true version." He gives a halfhearted, almost embarrassed laugh and uses a small twig to dig dirt out of a crack in the planter.

I don't know what to say. "How about both? Then I can pick the one I like."

Will takes a deep breath that seems to erase all the banker out of him. Suddenly, he's not a banker or a teacher or anything like that, he's just a person. A person, I suddenly realize, who is thousands of miles from home. I can't imagine what that feels like. I've been surrounded by home and family from my first breath.

"I tell Mom," he says, sticking the twig resolutely into the planter's bare soil, "that an international résumé is important in today's financial market and that I'm gaining vital business experience." It sounds rehearsed. Dry. Forced. Something twists in my chest.

"And when Mom's not around?"

After a moment, Will folds his hands and says very quietly, "It was the most distance I could put between my father and me."

Ouch. I turn to look at him, but he seems unwilling—afraid, maybe—to stare anywhere but straight ahead. I notice his fingers are laced together in a tight, tense knot. "What did you fight about?" I ask carefully.

Will shakes his head and attempts to laugh it off, but his words have far too much edge. "Everything. Life. Religion. Money, mostly."

"All families fight." I angle myself to face him. "Not all families need an ocean between them. What happened?"

"Do you always pry like this?" His tone is defensive, but you can just see in the way he holds his body that he *needs* to talk about this. It's eating at him, plain as day.

"Hey, I got three brothers. I'm an expert."

Will's shoulders are so rigid he looks ready for battle. "Dad was what you Americans would call an idea man. Mom called him a dreamer. All I could ever see out of him were schemes." There is enough bitterness in his words to taint all of Puget Sound. He waits for the rumble of a passing bus to subside before he continues. "My Mom came from money, from a good family. Respectable. My Dad did, too. Everyone thought they were such a smart match until Dad began to run through nearly every dime they had. Strings of sure-to-succeed ideas that proved only to be expensive failures." Will looks out over the water, but you can tell he's seeing England in his eyes, not Seattle. "I imagine he's hard at work on his latest as we speak." He picks up the twig he planted earlier and snaps it in half.

"You don't talk?" It seems obvious. I don't know why I asked.

"Mom and I stopped discussing Dad after I left. We only argue when we talked about him anyway." Will throws the twig halves onto the sidewalk. "I send her money every month. The checks keep getting cashed, so I can only assume Dad's still…at it."

I fight the urge to put my hand on his shoulder. Actually, I'm afraid to move; Will has let me in much further than he was planning to and the moment is alarmingly fragile.

"You know," he says, his voice losing some of the cold edge I just heard, "I believe that's the first time I've spoken of him since I moved here." He turns to me for the first time in our conversation, his eyes steel and sapphire—sharp and deep. "Do you do that to everyone?" he says, but there's not an ounce of teasing in his voice. He's dead serious. Intensity personified. "You are…so—" he seems to struggle for the right word "—surprising."

Oh, my.

"Yeah, well that's one way of putting it. I've heard it put…shall we say, in a less kindly manner?"

"Such as?" A hint of lightness returns to his voice, and his stance softens a bit.

"Weird. Odd. Creepy. Strange. With three brothers, I'm a walking thesaurus of annoying-sister adjectives." I shoot him a sideways glance. "Do you always drive people to make up lists of words?"

Will shrugs—an honest, almost boyish response that is neither banker nor teacher, but something of the rugby player shooting up through all that formal business demeanor.

"Hey," I venture, "you want to go get a burger at Dick's? You can't get more uncomplicated American than that." Visualize the quintessential drive-in all-night burger stand and that would be Dick's. It's a Seattle institution: grease, beef, cheese and pure deliciousness. One of those places that's at its best late at night.

It would take a dozen pages to describe the look on his face. Warmth and reserve and caution all warring in those eyes. Does he realize he's practically falling off the planter?

He wants to.

Chapter Fourteen

The lamest, most adorable waste of whipped cream

For a heart-stopping moment I watched Will teeter on the edge of his reserve, but then that man shut down so fast I was waiting for an audible alarm to go off.

"I'm not so sure that would be a good idea, Maggie." His voice is completely controlled, a hundred-and-eighty-degree turn from where he was mere seconds ago. Instantaneous male lockdown. How do they do that? "I shouldn't have come here."

"No," I counter, "that's not true. I'm glad you came. I'm glad we talked. And it's late. I need to get home anyway." I fumble my words, duped by the emotional whiplash I didn't see coming. "My cholesterol and my hips should both thank you for your sensibility. Diane says I'm always doing stupid stuff and staying out too late and…" Oh, great. Now I'm rambling. Like this isn't awkward enough as it is.

Will stands. "Let me make sure you get to your car safely."

My car is, um, twenty feet away. "Sure." I grab my apron and handbag and we walk for six, maybe seven seconds. "Yep, I'm here, all safe and sound." What a ridiculous thing to say.

"Indeed." Will laughs, sort of.

I am cringing in gargantuan proportions on the inside, smiling entirely too widely on the outside. "Thanks for the escort." Oh, I should just stop talking altogether. I'm making it worse with every word.

Will's still laughing softly. I picture him writing home about the crazy American woman he has to teach who won't stop talking and has absolutely no sense of decorum whatsoever. "At your service." He says. How come he can be clever and I just get to be stupid? "Good night."

"'Night."

I stopped banging my head against the steering wheel after I counted to twenty. My brothers were right: *weird, odd, creepy, strange.*

"Hi, Aunt Maggie!" Cathy and Charlie come into the coffee shop just after 3:00 p.m. Charlie, freshly sprung from school, still looks like a bundle of energy. He pivots upon entering the store, showing off his shiny new backpack with six-year-old pride. Cathy shuffles in behind him, looking like she wishes her bundle of energy still took naps. Charlie tears across the floor to launch himself onto a stool and plant his elbows on the counter. "You work here now?" His spanking-new white sneakers swing wildly on his chubby legs.

"Yep." I lean across the counter to give him a big kiss. "Your usual, Mister Big-time First Grader?"

"They got it here?" he marvels. Charlie always gets Aunt Mags' hot cocoa and a chocolate chip cookie at my house. I'm pretty sure I can tweak the corporate version to his liking.

"Hi, Maggie," Cathy calls as she slips onto the stool next to Charlie. We make some small talk while I gather my ingredients. Suddenly, Cathy cracks an odd smile. "So...um...hey, little sister, what's the strongest tasting decaf you can whip me up?" She gives "decaf" extra emphasis.

"Decaf? Since when do you...?" I stop cold. There's only one reason in the world my big sister would forgo her favorite caffeine and her grin gives her away in two seconds. I'm tearing around the counter to hug the stuffing out of her when Charlie yells "I'm getting a baby sister Aunt Maggie!"

"So I figured out!" I call out from the tangle of arms and legs that is hugging Cathy and Charlie together. "Cath, that's great. When?"

"February."

"Near Valentine's Day," spouts a ridiculously proud Charlie from over her shoulder.

"Well," I reply, making no attempts to keep my

enthusiasm down to corporate standards. "We gotta whip us up some special drinks for a special occasion like this." I wink at Charlie. "But, first graders always come first. "And up!" I hold up a mug, beginning the hot-chocolate ritual I share with each of my nieces and nephews. Like I said, I was born to be doing this kind of thing.

"And in!" Charlie replies as I pour a huge portion of chocolate syrup into the mug.

"And in!" I add the milk. Whole milk. None of this skim stuff for my kiddos.

"And under!" Charlie shouts, making his own version of the cappuccino machine's trademark whoosh sound as I steam the milk. Once it's hot enough (but never too hot), I set the mug down in front of him and we stare at each other for a long, anticipatory pause.

"And now…" I say quietly in my best suspense-filled voice.

"And now…" Charlie echoes loudly.

"And now…" I draw the whipped-cream canister like John Wayne at a shoot-out. "On top!" I start with a sensible dollop of whipped cream.

"Oh, no!" Charlie yelps, on cue.

"Oh, no!" I reply with mock alarm. "It's broke!"

The whipped cream canister, as I'm guessing you've figured out by now, suddenly malfunctions, leaving Charlie with a drink that is more topping than beverage. I don't put a saucer under that mug for nothing—it's oozing over the top long before I'm done. Charlie's squealing with delight.

Works every time. Let's just say I go through a lot of whipped cream at my house. I take my most-favored aunt status very seriously.

I expected this store to be bustling most of the time. It isn't. There are times when I am downright bored. I hadn't counted on that. Which is why after I send my sister off—filled with the most delectable decaf drink I can produce—and the squall of words that is my nephew Charlie has left, the store is completely empty. Nate, who has kindly taken all customers over the last twenty minutes so I can fawn over Cathy and Charlie and their wonderful news, stares at me for a long moment.

Now, I'd be the first person to tell you Nate's a handsome guy, but our relationship is pure friendship. No zing. It's more like a brother-sister thing than any kind of office romance.

"You're kidding," he says, with a look of complete disbelief.

"About what?" Although I can guess.

"The whipped cream thing. That's got to be the lamest, inexcusable, most adorable waste of whipped cream I have ever seen. Kids must follow you like you were Mary Poppins."

Forgetting that Mary Poppins had questionable taste in fashion and a talking umbrella, I choose to accept the compliment. I wipe the counter with a tiny air of smugness. "Works on more than just kids, you know. I've seen grown women fall for that and love every minute of it."

"No. Not in a million years." He shifts his weight to one hip and crosses his arms doubtfully.

Now, you don't want to put me in that kind of competitive position. I've got three brothers. Daring is a highly effective motivation strategy with someone like me. If you can't see the dare in Nate's eyes when he says that, then you need glasses. "Oh," I say, glaring right back, "you'd be amazed. It's one of my very best tricks." I point at him with my rag, knowing exactly what I am about to unleash. "Even you could pull it off."

Nate shakes his head. "Not a chance."

Two minutes of coaching later, a very pretty young woman walks through the door. Nate starts pulling her drink with loads of charm. Let's just say that Nate's strength is definitely "customer relations." Poor thing, she will never know what hit her.

"Do you want whipped cream on that?"

Our young lady stifles a flirty giggle. "Maybe just a smidge." I'm pretty sure she winked. I shoot a sideways glance at Nate as he finishes pulling her drink. I'm pretending to arrange scones. He reaches down into the fridge below the counter for the whipped cream dispenser and proceeds to put the tiniest dollop of whipped cream ever on her drink. He catches my eye for a split second, then goes into action. Suddenly the whipped cream dispenser "malfunctions."

"Whoa!" Nate exclaims as the top of her cup fills with billows of whipped cream. "Sorry about that.

I'll pull another skim mocha for you if you want, but…" He doesn't finish the sentence, but picks up the drink and holds it toward her. He flashes the kind of smile that could make women exit a shoe sale to follow him into a hardware store.

"Oh, no," she coos, a look of unconscious delight on her face. "I wouldn't make you do that. I'll just take it…as is." She saunters—no kidding, that's exactly the word I'd use for it—out of the store.

After she leaves, Nate leans against the sink throws his hands up in surrender. "Wow. You're good."

"Intuition. Barista life skill."

"And here my mom always told me it was a woman thing."

I smile. "It is, but its coffee applications can be learned by students with a…certain aptitude."

"Gimme some of that aptitude."

"Patience, my young friend." My Yoda impression leaves much to be desired. He gets it anyway and laughs. "Seriously," I say, "you have to be able to tell who really wants you to skimp on the whipped cream and who's just kidding themselves. It's all in how they ask. Anyone who uses the word *smidge* is a sure-fire candidate."

"You're too good for Carter's," Nate says straightening the bottles on the counter behind us. "You should open your own place.

You know, I *knew* there was a reason I liked Nate so much.

Chapter Fifteen

Just one more shot

"You should open your own place."

Those words echoed in my head the entire afternoon, like a blessed affirmation. As the sun went down, though, doubts crept in with the shadows. Am I really doing what God wants? Or just seeing what I want to see through the filter of my own ambition? I think of David, loading his slingshot to take down the giant. He trusted God to help him beat the monumental odds against him. I feel the same way.

Then I remember David didn't exactly play it squeaky clean once he grew up. Would I ever let my success drown out my ability to hear God? *If You told me to abandon Higher Grounds, Lord, would I even listen?* What separates single-minded devotion from self-serving obsession?

As if feeding on its own doubts, my mind turns to Will. *Why send me a highly attractive yet out-of-bounds Englishman with serious family baggage? Why am I always wondering what Will Grey is doing? I thought I was on my way to my ministry, but instead everything is feeling so out of place.*

And a tea drinker? Is this Your idea of a joke?

I don't know if I was expecting the answer to appear on the bottom of my prayer journal page, but my pen stays still, my page doesn't fill and I am still confused. Maybe I need to go on retreat or something. Climb a mountain with only a thermos of coffee, my journal and a Bible.

My contemplation is cut short by the phone ringing.

"You free Saturday morning?" Diane often thinks of herself as my social secretary. Most women might find that annoying but, sadly, I need her. Outside of family stuff, I'm never busy. Diane always whips up something for me to do.

"What's up?"

"I'm taking photos for this guy's CD cover. Christian acoustic Folk. Deep, faith-filled…"

"And exceedingly handsome?" I finish for her. Diane's loyal and fun-loving, but a little predictable.

"Adorable. I need someone to hold the lights if it's windy."

"Sure. I actually don't have to work Saturday." I dump the basket of white laundry—this job has me wearing every white shirt I own—onto my bed and start folding with the phone wedged between my shoulder and my ear.

"I'll pick you up at nine. Oh, and wear sensible shoes. We're shooting out at Sand Point on the Art Walk."

Let's just hope I can get through a trip to Sand Point without a visit to the emergency room this time.

"Turn a little toward me. Drop the guitar about six inches. There we go. That's it." Diane's camera whirs through half a dozen shots. This was fun for about twenty minutes. Now, it's tedious. I'm essentially a human lamp, holding something that looks like a cross between a lightbulb and an umbrella, watching Mr. Deep and Faithful's hair blow compellingly in the breeze.

Sure, I'll buy his CD.

If it means I can stop holding all this hardware.

"Di," I murmur out of Mr. Deep and Faithful's earshot, "are you going for perfection or just seeing how much time you can stare at him through the camera lens?" Sometimes, I question why Diane took up photography in the first place. Was it really for the art? Or just for the ogling?

"Just one more shot," Diane pleads with squinted eyes. "Maybe two."

"It was 'maybe two' half an hour ago. I know patience is a virtue, but can I stop playing light fixture now?"

Diane tries to glare at me. It can't work, though, because she realizes I'm already onto her attempts to play this little scenario out as long as possible. Now she can't stare me down. "Fine," she concedes. "We won't need the light if I just do ambient-light close-ups anyhow. Go take a walk or something and I'll ring your cell when we're ready to go."

When she's ready to go? I can probably find a coffee bar, drink three cups and read the morning paper by the time she's "ready to go." Ambient-light close-ups. *Please.* I hear her cooing to the guy to turn toward the sun as I wander out past the large-scale outdoor art that adorns Sand Point's Magnuson Park. The morning is cool and clear; people are already on the Kite Hill flying colorful masterpieces. I keep walking down the Art Walk, no particular destination in mind, just glad not to be holding something upright for minutes on end.

I must have been meandering for twenty minutes or so, my thoughts directed more inward than on the scenery. "Whazza matter, sunshine, leave your game face at home today?" A growling Aussie accent pierces the morning air—and my thoughts.

Oh, no.

A chorus of grunts and the sound of general male mayhem echoes from up over the hill.

Magnuson Park. Sand Point. The athletic fields. Rugby practice. Will.

I make a Lord, You're-not-serious? face toward heaven and scramble my way up the hill just in time to see Arthur Sumners thrust himself into what looks like a pile of grizzly humanity. I look at the locked circle of arms and legs, twitching and moving down the field like some kind of multi-legged ambulatory wrestling amoeba. Whoever called it a *maul* had a good gift for description.

Oh, no, you don't. My stomach is absolutely *not* allowed to do that little flippy thing because *he's* here.

But he *is* here. He stands out from the other guys, mud and all, as he runs down the field or pitch or whatever it is they call it. You know, when women get dirty, we look…well…dirty. How come when men get dirty, they look all rugged and handsome? We don't look like that when our hair gets mussed up. We look mussed up. He looks…oh, let's not go there.

"Will you look at that? I'm bleeding again. Why am I always bleeding?" Arthur moans to his teammates.

"Must be all that time you spend grinding your face into the ground." Will fishes a handkerchief out of his shorts pocket and hands it to Art. A handkerchief. Come on, when's the last time you saw anyone use one of those? Okay, anyone under fifty?

It's no big deal. I'll just slip back down the hill before anyone sees me. We all know what happened the last time I got anywhere near…

He saw me. Did you see that? His whole body went still the minute he saw me. He's fifty yards away and I still feel it under my skin. Great. If I walk away now, I'll look like I'm running. If I stand still, I'll look stupid. I've got to walk toward him. Oh, closer is not exactly where I want to be right now.

Couldn't they start the game up now or something? Urgent rugby business and all?

Will jogs up the hill toward me. "I can't seem to stop running into you. Fancy that," he pants breathlessly, bending over a bit and wiping the grime off his face.

"Yeah. Fancy that." Oh, stunning Maggie. Just stunning.

"Well, I know you're not turning in a paper. Out for a walk?" He flicks some grass out of his hair.

"I'm helping my friend Diane take some photographs." I can't remember what I threw on for clothes this morning. Do I have earrings in? No, you fool, don't reach up and check. Look casual. Cas-u-al. "I got tired of holding her equipment. Are you winning or losing?"

Will cocks his head back toward the team. "The lads? We haven't started playing yet. The game's in half an hour or so. We're just warming up."

"By inflicting injury? Aren't you supposed to stay clean until the starting pitch or whatever?"

Will cracks a disarming smile. "Funny. Starting *kick,* by the way. Besides, there's no clean in rugby."

"So I see."

"Hey Romeo, we've got a match in twenty. Think you can save the flirting for afterwards?" Art's baritone booms across the grass.

"I've…well…you know."

I wave him off. "What ho the lads and all. Go beat each other up and have fun."

Will starts down the hill. Three steps into it, he turns back. "You could stay and watch…that is…if you'd like." It's as if he's almost embarrassed to ask.

"Hey, we all know how it turned out the last time. I'm just all healed. Wouldn't want to risk it. Besides, I gotta get back to Diane." *Liar.*

"Of course."

"Grey!" Another teammate calls out impatiently.

"Have fun," I say as Will waves and jogs off down the hill.

That. That hum in my stomach. Why does that have to happen with Will Grey of all people?

Chapter Sixteen

The trouble with brilliant theories

"So," Will says, writing two words on the classroom whiteboard, "the biggest question facing most of you is where to spend and where to save." He underlines *spend* and *save* where he's written them in crisp, precise capital letters. "I'm going to tell you a story."

Will Grey? Spinning tales? This is a new one.

"A real-estate broker was unimpressed with his success. He'd furnished a posh office for his high-end clientele, had brochures and business cards printed up, hired a secretary to answer his calls and focused his considerable talents on finding new business. He did well, but not as well as he wanted. After three months of pondering the problem, our hero sacked his secretary, closed his office, bought a powerful laptop computer, launched a Web site and leased a top-of-the-line Mercedes Benz with every luxury option made. For the next month he ran his businesses essentially from that car, without the benefit of desk or secretary. He tripled his business by the end of the year." Will sits on the desk. "Why?"

"Internet," replies Josh Mason. "It's the marketplace of the future for everything, I'm telling you." Did anyone really expect cyber-guy to have any other answer?

"Correct, in part. But I'm looking for a bigger answer here."

Jerry Davis hoists a chunky little hand. I think Will's told him five times that he doesn't have to raise his hand; this isn't eighth grade. He still raises his hand and waits for Will to call on him. Will does. "He lowered his overhead. No rent, no employees, higher profits."

Will nods at Jerry. "You're getting closer. But you're all still just looking at parts of the picture and missing the whole. Think, ladies and gentlemen, think bigger."

It dawns on me. A light bulb just lit up over my head. "He put his money in the right places," I offer. "Real-estate brokers are always driving people around in their cars. A fancy car connotes success. No one cares about a broker's office, because by the time they're in there to sign the papers he's already hooked them as a customer anyway. Plus, now he's constantly mobile, so he's always out in the field where the business—and the customers—are." I get it. I finally get it! I've always been passionate about reaching people, but this is the first time I'm catching the craving for building a strong *business*. I think this is what Will was aiming for all along— to match business skills with my desire to fulfill my mission. That "doing it as unto the Lord" also means getting the business end—that numbers element—right, because a strong business can reach further, last longer and do more. What do you know? The William Grey numbers fever is actually contagious.

"Yes!" Will shouts. I've never heard him shout in class before. There's this moment, this stop-the-clocks moment, where the room hums. Our eyes lock onto each other and…I don't know how else to put this: he knows I know. He gets that I get it. I feel like I just downed a quintuple-shot Americano with extra sugar.

"It's not always about economy or efficiency." He continues after what seems like a huge pause. Did anyone else notice what just happened? They all look pretty normal to me. Josh is typing at blinding speed, Jerry just looks confused. Every one else in the class seems oblivious to the connection I just felt. Will and I are staring at each other, while trying not to stare at each other. "It's not always about where to cut your costs." Okay, that's the first time I've ever heard Will repeat himself in class. He clears his throat. I find something interesting on my shoe. "We often think of spending only what we need. There are places in every business where spending more than what you need—splurging, if you will—may mean the difference between a mediocre business and a successful one. Excellence. Don't just meet your customer's expectations, *exceed* them. And you must know where the money should go to make that happen."

Will points to another class member. "Miss Rockhurst," he says as he moves to stand right in front of her. "Where's a place to splurge in your store?"

Linda Rockhurst, who wants to open a housewares boutique, thinks for a moment. "Bed sheets." She says, her meek voice gaining a bit of confidence. "If they feel absolutely fabulous, some people will pay anything for them."

Will spins to face Jerry. "What's the single most important ingredient in your pasta sauce?"

"That's easy," Jerry replies, almost chuckling. "Tomatoes."

"Then job number one for you is finding the absolute best tomatoes in Seattle. On the whole West Coast, for that matter. Are they expensive?"

"You'd better believe it," quips Jerry. It's the closest thing to a joke he's made all class.

"And, people, is that a good place for Mr. Davis to put a lot of money?"

"Yes." We all reply in chorus.

Will beams. Positively beams.

"Maggie, will your customers care what's on your cups?"

Of course. I certainly care. It's tantamount to

traveling advertising. And traveling advertising means more people get to experience Higher Grounds. "Yes, that's where my logo goes."

"Mr. Mason," Will spins toward Josh again. "Think about the last time you had a cup of coffee at somewhere other than a chain. What was on the cup?"

Josh thinks for a moment. "I have no idea."

Will snaps both fingers. "Classic. Absolutely classic." His excitement could light the room. "That's not saying there isn't a time to invest in custom-printed cups for Higher Grounds, but it isn't now. Now is all about the…the what? What matters most to your coffeehouse?"

I open my mouth to answer.

"Besides the beans," he interrupts, his voice nearly playful.

It's not even the beans—although they're important. I don't even have to think for a second. "The espresso machine." I can see that baby in my mind right now. The gleaming metal. The perfectly aligned levers and cups. The sound of steam so sweet it's like a melody.

"And a top-of-the-line machine runs you…? He stands at the whiteboard, having already written the dollar sign, waiting to fill in the number.

"Um…more than my current car, that's for sure."

He looks mildly surprised. He probably has a ten-dollar coffeemaker—if that—in his home. Maybe just a six-dollar teakettle. "Specifically?"

"Fourteen thousand dollars. For the absolute

finest, you'd pay fourteen thousand. And you might have to buy two to keep up with rush hour."

You can tell that's absolutely not the answer he was looking for. It's a huge percentage of my start-up costs. He hesitates before writing down the number I just gave him. It's too much. He'd never condone my spending that kind of money, even though he just spent the last half an hour telling us to spend that kind of money. I told you I'm always breaking the rules. I just blew a hole in his theory, in his whole lesson. I can see his gears turning, trying to figure out how to cope with the exception—my exception—to his brilliant theory. He can't just turn around and say "Except if we're talking about espresso machines, in which case frugal mediocrity will just have to do."

He turns around to face the class. "Well, it certainly does give one food for thought, doesn't it?" All the passion, all the energy of the last twenty minutes has evaporated, replaced by the crisp, reserved banker we've had all along.

Want to tell me what just happened? Because I have no idea.

We just had this amazing connection—Will and I—followed by a bucket of ice water. I'm reeling, and I think he is, too. I've messed up his math, and I'm feeling bad about it even though it's no fault of my own. Not because I don't like being the exception to every rule—actually, I find that role lots of fun. It's the palpable lack of excitement that now fills the room. The deflated moment. A huge case of unspoken, psychological oh, well, never mind.

I hate it. Why do I hate it?

Because I caused it. Or, at least, I *feel* like I caused it. Because money just got in the way of mission. Again.

Chapter Seventeen

The obvious under pressure

Will wrapped up class in an efficient six minutes and is presently stomping back to his office. Oh, no, you don't. You don't get to do that to my insides and then stomp away mad. I didn't set the price for fine espresso hardware. You can't take this out on me. Not now. Not after what I just figured out.

"Will!" I run down the hall after him, not caring that I've just used his first name in public. He doesn't even turn around. I'm not letting him get away. I hurl myself around the corner and catch his elbow. "Just slow down a minute, will you?"

He turns, his face unreadable.

"You're mad at me." Yes, folks, I can usually be counted on to state the obvious when under pressure. Pressure is what makes good espresso, but it's not what makes good Maggie Black.

"I most certainly am not." He starts walking again. Give me a break; a more obvious statement of untruth has never existed.

"It's not my fault espresso machines are so expensive, you know." I start after him, almost running to keep up with his agitated strides. "Why is it okay for everyone else to splurge but not me? Jerry's tomatoes are worth their weight in gold but *I* have to make do with a mediocre espresso machine?"

"I never said that." Will turns the corner into his office.

"You didn't have to. It was all over your face." I follow right behind.

He plants his books on his credenza. "Why must you be so aggravating?"

"I'm not. You started it." Juvenile as that sounds, it's absolutely true. "*You* posed the theory about when it makes sense to buy the very best. You asked me how much the machines cost. I told you. Then you got mad. How is that my fault?"

Will whips his tie off. "It's not. You, standing in my office, picking a fight about it—*that's* entirely your doing."

"Because you got mad."

"I did not get mad," he growls. "I reacted. I expressed my...surprise."

"If that's how Englishmen show their surprise, then remind me never to throw you a surprise party."

"I highly doubt that's an issue."

"Fine."

"Fine."

He stares at me. I am not leaving.

Will crosses his arms and leans against his desk. I lean against the door. I push out a huge breath and put my handbag and books down. "Round two," I say, forcing calm into my voice. "Why was the price such a problem?"

I see him force the same calm into his voice. "A coffeemaker really costs fourteen thousand dollars? And you need two of them?"

"It's not a coffeemaker. That twelve dollar hardware-store purchase on your kitchen counter? *That's* a coffeemaker. This is a precision industrial instrument. It's practically a work of art. Handmade. By world-famous guys in Italy. I could get by with one, but not if the location has a drive-through. I'm not crazy about drive-throughs, but if that's what the research says people want, then I guess I need to have one."

He's impressed I'm actually doing research. For that matter, *I'm* impressed I'm actually doing research. Still, his expression holds solid doubt. "It's a huge percentage of your loan request."

I slide into his guest chair. "Actually, the way I see it, my loan request will be larger after this class. There's a lot I didn't take into consideration."

"I've been trying to make you see that all along," he groans.

"So why is an expensive machine a problem if you say it'll lead to excellence in my coffee shop?"

"Because your coffee shop is already a huge risk. Pinning so much capital on one piece of equipment doesn't make sense for you."

I don't buy that one. "But it does for everyone else?"

"Everyone else is not facing the same odds you are."

I don't buy that one, either. "God specializes in the tough cases. I'm not worried. How can I make you see that I'm not worried about that kind of stuff?"

I suddenly see it. Partly satisfying, partly sickening, and completely clear: "You're protecting me."

Yep. Did you see that look? I'm on to him. He probably didn't even realize it himself. His features darken. No doubt about it; that's the last thing he wanted to hear.

Will has no answer for that. He makes an exasperated sound, pushes himself up off the side of the desk and sits down behind it. As if he needs something solid between us.

I'm not backing down now. This isn't about coffee or machines or math or money. This is about something far more important and if I don't ask the real question, we're never going to get to the real discussion. "Why are you protecting me? Why am I the exception to the rule?"

"You're not."

"I am," I blast back, coming up on the edge of my seat.

"You most certainly are not."

"I am and you know I am."

Will throws his hands up in the air. "Fine. Fine. You win. You are."

I sit back.

"I can't look at your case objectively," Will blurts out. "I'm worried about you and I want to protect you. There. I said it. Are you satisfied?"

"We need to talk about this." Unoriginal, granted, but my brain's going a hundred miles an hour right now.

"Aren't we doing that?"

The sort of helpless, cornered look on his face makes my pulse skip. A warm, gooey kind of skip that makes it impossible to stay angry at this aggravating man. "Look, we can argue about budgets and formulas all you want, but I think we need to talk about something entirely different." In a fit of bravery, I add, "And you know what it is. And we'd better figure out what to do about it."

Will stares at me. My pulse goes past skipping and stops altogether. His eyes look vibrant and powerful—like thunderclouds, both frightening and dazzling at the same time. After a long moment, he says, "Are you sure that's a good idea?"

You know, I've had it with his confounded British reserve. "Since when is this kind of thing ever a good idea? And there is a *this kind of thing,* Will. Let's not even try to pretend there isn't."

"That's dangerous ground, Maggie."

Fidgety, I get up out of the chair. "Yes, I know what you said after that rugby tutorial." I'm pacing.

When did I start pacing? "But it isn't going away, is it? We keep ending up around each other even when we say we won't. I know we've said this is too risky to let happen, but I've got news for you, William Grey III, it's *already* happened. So what are we going to do about it?" I pick one of the dozen arranged pencils up off his desk and start twirling it in my fingers.

Will stands up to grab my twitching hands and snatch the pencil from them. "Then maybe we should try harder to stop it." Suddenly, he realizes he's holding my hands. He yanks them back, stuffing them into his jacket pockets.

"Why?"

"I think that should be obvious."

"Bankers shouldn't date their customers. Yes, I'm sure there's some handbook with a whole chapter on that. Okay, so *why* shouldn't bankers date their customers?"

"Conflict of interest," He practically shouts.

"That's my call, isn't it? As for me, there's no conflict. I'm interested. It's weird, it's not at all what I had in mind, but there it is. I'm interested. You're interested. We can find a solution for the business issues when it comes to that. Let's let things get interesting and see what happens."

Will looks a bit stunned. That might have been a bit too direct, even for me. "Look," he replies, "it's not just 'your call.' The bank needs to make sure an objective decision gets made. I thought we could just be careful about this but it's not working. I'm afraid we'll end up doing something we'll both regret. And I won't let that happen."

It's there, all over his face. He's made up his mind. Even if I want to cross this line, to take this enormous risk, it won't happen. That hurts worse than any rejection he could have handed me. I yank Will's office door open. It pops out of me before I can stop it. "Worth all the protection but none of the risk. You don't want to protect me, you want to protect *yourself.*"

I grab my bag and my books and walked out of there as fast as I can, waiting for some kind of reaction from him. Waiting, with some small tender part of me, for him to come after me and stop me.

He never said a word.

I cried when I got home.

It made me furious that I did, but I couldn't seem to stop. Stupid, isn't it? I feel horrible and I feel worse for feeling horrible.

I ranted to God about the whole mess. I railed to Him about how hurt and confused I felt. I pleaded for clarity and wisdom. By the end of an hour I was reduced to begging Him to make the whole thing go away.

No responses came to me.

The long shower didn't help. Nor the two *I Love Lucy* reruns. So why am I surprised when the entire package of chocolate-chip cookies fails to grant me any answers?

It's after midnight and I'm prayed out. There's

no hope for this tonight. I might as well sleep on it and see what the morning brings.

I'm just throwing away the pathetically empty cookie bag when my doorbell rings. Great. That's the third time this year Diane has locked herself out of her apartment when she gets off the evening shift at the hospital. I yawn and pad over to the door, reaching for the spare set of Diane's keys that I keep in a bowl nearby.

My eyeball practically glues itself to the peephole.

It's Will.

His shirt's untucked; his tie and jacket are gone. He's just standing there, hands in his pockets, looking supremely uncomfortable. He looks *mussed.*

I gulp—probably loud enough for him to hear on the other side of my door, paw pointlessly through my hair, check my face for chocolate smudges and open the door.

"Hullo," he says softly.

I lean my head against the door. "Hi, Will."

"I…well…I don't like how we left off. May I come in?"

Chapter Eighteen

Our side of the pond

"Sure. I'll put a pot of..." I was going to say I'll put a pot of coffee on, but somehow that seems like the last thing I should do. "Why don't you just come on in?"

I pull the door wide open and Will steps inside. "Thanks."

A sour feeling about my last remark to him—the feeling that's churned in my stomach for the last couple of hours—rises and tightens in my chest. "Hey, look, I shot my mouth off and..."

Will looks at me. "Don't."

"No, really, I'm sorry. It's just that this is so incredibly...awkward? Difficult? Weird? Take your pick. I'm at a loss here." I motion toward my kitchen.

Will takes a deep breath as he pulls out a kitchen

chair and sits down. "Actually, I was thinking it was quite the opposite."

"Huh?"

"Well, it seemed to me that you knew exactly what you wanted to do. I'm the one who seems to be saying one thing and doing another."

I don't know who he's kidding—I haven't the slightest idea what I'm doing. I'm making this up as I go along. The television chatters softly from the living room and I can hear the ice-maker release its cubes inside my freezer. It's that quiet between us. I walk over to the fridge. "You want something to drink?" I say to fill the gap of silence.

"No. I'm fine, thanks." He looks up to catch my eyes, suddenly looking older than he did mere hours ago. "Or rather, I'm not at all fine. I don't like how we left off."

I guess we're getting right into it then, without the pleasantries. I suppose that's best. I sit down, my fingers fiddling with the ribbon edge of the place mats I got at last year's flea market. "I'm sorry about what I said." It seems like the best place to start, because I am. It was a lousy thing to say.

"Don't be. You spoke your mind. I'm the one who hasn't been fair." His face lightens just a bit, still tired but gaining warmth. "Although," he shakes his head, "I must admit, you are far more direct than I ever counted on."

The corner of my mouth creeps up. "America's a pretty in-your-face nation. And," I sigh, "I'm a pretty in-your-face person from an equally in-your-

face family. Even the natives find me a bit intense."
I flatten my hands on the table to stop my infernal
fidgeting. "I do owe you an apology for railing at
you like that. You've been trying to do the right
thing and I blasted you for it. It's just that I got
excited when I finally understood the whole
business thing. Then when it all fell to pieces…" I
gesture vaguely, unable to describe the tornado of
emotions that was tonight's class and its aftermath.

"It did. And I'm sorry about that." Even though
Will looks beat, it gives him an unfettered sort of
calm. As if he's too spent to put up the usual front.
"Some things are going on at the bank. There's a
lot of…pressure right now." Will spreads his hands
on the table. "Look, Maggie, it was never my intent
to hurt you. But surely you must realize that I'm not
the kind of man who can ignore the rules." His
voice is different, and I realize I'm seeing Will Grey
let down his guard. Intentionally.

"Are you sure there are rules, Will?" I say carefully, "Worthwhile rules?"

"I want you to know you…you *do* mean something to me. That I wish circumstances were different. I know you want me to dive into this," Will
continues. "Ignore the consequences, toss every
rule to the contrary and start up with you. But can
you see that you're asking me to jeopardize your financial future just because…?" he doesn't even
finish the sentence.

I lean my head on one hand and out of the corner
of my eye I catch the microwave clock click over

to 1:01 a.m. "Would it help you to know I'm not exactly sure what I want?" That's absolutely true. I don't do casual. I fling myself full-force into relationships, which is why I've got a hit parade of heartbreaks to show for it. I don't know how to deal with anything requiring this much caution.

Will clears his throat. "I don't know what to do. The right thing would be if we simply didn't talk to each other outside of class." He rakes his fingers through his hair. "And I keep saying I'm going to do that, but I don't seem quite able to follow through." When his eyes land on mine, they seem a murky, heathered blue. Like the fog the morning after a storm. "I enjoy your company, Maggie. Immensely. But, I don't want to make promises I shouldn't keep or give you possibilities you shouldn't consider."

"I'm a big girl, Will," I reply, pushing out my breath and returning his questioning glance. "I know this isn't a clear-cut situation. I'm not ready to rush through this door, but I'm also not ready to slam it shut." I hold his gaze. "I don't think you are either or you wouldn't be here. You'd be leaving some vaguely negative 'it's not you, it's me' message on my answering machine."

Will frowns his disapproval. "Is *that* the conduct of the average American male?"

I chuckle. "At least the ones I've had the pleasure of meeting."

He takes on a very serious look. "That's not something I'd ever do."

"I know that." And I do. Just by the way he acts. This guy has a sense of honor—okay, maybe a little overblown into a protective-hero-complex, but honor just the same—that you just don't see much. Never, actually. The idea surfaces with a quiet pop, like a bubble. "I think I might know where to start. Have coffee with me. Let me show you what a top-flight espresso machine can do. If you still hate it, I'll shut up and you'll never hear about it from me again. But you need to taste what this thing can do."

"Maggie…"

"Think of it as business research, if that makes it easier. Me flexing my very fine salesmanship skills here. One cup of coffee. Actually, three—I want to make you an espresso, a cappuccino and a latte."

He wants to. And me? I want to be the one to brew the cup of coffee that wins Will Grey over.

"That's hardly a good place to start." His words offer resistance, but there is no conviction in his voice.

"It's the best place to start, Will. Look at it this way—you're the ultimate wrong customer. You're the hardest sell I'll ever have in setting up this business. It's valuable experience for me to show you—to *sell* you on the machine."

I can see the willingness hiding inside his eyes. Just a speck of silver in all that murky blue, but like a shiny dime at the bottom of a fountain, it glints for all the world to see.

I resort to the last weapon I have.

"Come on, Will, I dare you. Three cups of coffee. It's the only way you can really evaluate my budget and the cost of those machines."

"Just three cups?" he turns the idea over in his mind, examining it.

"Not even three. More like two and a half, actually. Espressos are tiny."

He narrows his eyes. "You can show me the exact machines you want and why they're worth the price?"

"Absolutely." Well, I haven't asked my friend the executive chef for permission to work her machines, but we'll cover those tiny details later.

"And if I can't taste the difference, you'll consider a more moderately-priced set of machines."

"Yep." I put out a hand to shake on it.

Will takes my hand and the resulting *zing* could power half of Seattle. We keep our hands touching for several seconds too long, until Will pulls his hand back and runs it through his hair. "I have a strong feeling I'll regret this."

I grin. "Not a chance."

We fall awkwardly silent. Both our heads are spinning with the sensation of just touching, but neither of us is ready—or willing—to admit it out loud.

"Well," Will stands up and holds his other hand stiffly to his side as if it might misbehave if permitted free rein. "It's late. I've loads to do at the office tomorrow. Call me with the when and where of our meeting, then?"

I can't help but smile. "By noon. I've got the place in mind already and it'll just take a phone call to set it up."

"Right then."

"Right then."

"Good night."

I pull my door open and lean against it. "Good *morning,* William Grey III."

He laughs as he makes his way down my stairs.

Score one for our side of the pond.

Diane showed up at Carter's within thirty seconds of my Thursday's shift ending. I only called her four times yesterday. I thought that showed considerable restraint. You might even say British reserve. You know you're desperate to dish the dirt with someone when you'll even suggest going grocery shopping together.

"So," Diane says, pulling open the door the to QFC market, "you're having a three-beverage relationship? I know I said he's a nice guy and all, but do you really think you can do this, Maggie? He's told you he doesn't like coffee. He's not going to start now just because he thinks you're cute." She grabs two baskets and hands me one as the store loudspeaker announces how strawberries are currently buy one, get one free.

I shoot her a glare and draw an invisible box in the air. "Carefully drawn boundaries. That's the key here."

Diane picks up two containers of strawberries. "One of these is yours." We always share the buy-one, get-one-free offers when we can. She stares at me hard. "Maggie, watch yourself. You don't do limits. You don't do moderation. This can't end well. You like this guy too much."

I snag a bottle of coffee creamer and give Diane a direct look. "No, I think this is a smart move."

Diane gives me a do-you-really-want-to-know-what-I-think-of-that? look as we head off to toward the frozen food. "When's coffee hour anyway?" she asks with her head inside the freezer door. "You want to come over and heat up a pizza tonight?" She holds up a frozen pizza.

"No, I want to finish my homework for class. And *coffee hour,* as you so delicately put it, is Friday at three-thirty."

"So—" Diane smirks "—you've got a high-class place to take a high-class guy you're trying not to get too involved with to convince him over a beverage he doesn't like that you need a machine he doesn't think you can afford."

"Yes, that's it."

"Maggie Black, you are in trouble. Good thing this guy strikes me as noble. And Christian. And he has a dozen handsome, strapping male friends. I might be really worried otherwise."

"Ha!"

"Mags," Diane stops at the end of the aisle.

"Hmm?"

"I *am* worried. Have you prayed about this? Are you sure you know what you're doing?"

"Diane, I have no idea what I'm doing. I'm just taking this one cup at a time."

Chapter Nineteen

Do you know how I know?

Friday afternoon at three-thirty, I am standing in front of the most beautiful machine I've ever seen. A symphony of chrome, tubes and dials, it is so sleek it looks like it should have a hood ornament. Everything fits together with artistic precision. Every detail screams quality. I love these machines like other people love great art. I've only got forty-five minutes to share that love, because I had to promise the executive chef (who's both a friend of mine and the roommate of a girl my brother is currently dating) that Will and I would be out by the dinner rush.

I feel like the whole day is balancing on three cups of coffee.

Actually, I feel like my whole future is balancing on three cups of coffee.

I begin the process of explaining the machine—and it's many fine attributes—to Will. "Unlike your kitchen coffeemaker…"

"If I *had* a kitchen coffeemaker," Will interjects lightheartedly as he sits down at a nearby table.

"Unlike *a* kitchen coffeemaker," I correct myself, "the water needs to be boiling before you start. The water passes through the coffee grounds at high pressure. No air escapes. And the grounds are much finer than percolated or dripped coffee. That's why it tastes different."

"But I always hear a hissing sound." He comments. "Why?"

"Because steam is used to heat the milk. That way you get it hot without scalding the milk." I arrange three cups on the table in front of him, adopting my best salesmanship demeanor. "The strongest is the espresso. It's the pure stuff." I point to the smallest of the cups, which almost looks like it belongs in a child's tea set. "It's small because no one but the most hard-core caffeine junky would drink more than a couple of ounces. It's what is produced when the water is forced through very fine grounds. Nothing is added. High octane all the way." I point to the cup that looks like a regular coffee cup. "Next, we have the cappuccino, which isn't as strong, because you mix the espresso with steamed milk and it has this fabulous, rich foam on top. It's a different, more complex flavor. The latte," I say, pointing to the tall cup, "combines the same ingredients but in a different ratio and people make it in dozens of flavors. Each drink is distinct and you might like one more than the other."

"Or I might not like any." His eyes challenge me. He might not have actually spoken the words "I dare you," but his eyes are screaming it right now.

Megan, the executive chef who made this whole thing possible and who is standing behind me, chuckles at that. Even when I explained it a second time, she said she had no idea what it was I was doing.

Not to worry, though, because I know exactly what I'm doing. *Go ahead, your lordship, dare me. Double-dog dare me.* I am up to this challenge one hundred percent. I check the temperature gauge. "Just another minute or so," I say, disarmed by the anticipation I'm feeling. "I want this j-u-s-t right. These will be the best cups of coffee you've ever had."

"Worth every penny?"

"Splurge-worthy in every detail."

Megan offers a condescending look. "I'll just leave you two kids alone."

I glare at her, not appreciating her none-too-subtle insinuation.

"I've got a baked goods delivery coming in. I need to check through the order," she says, in a hey, I-just-call-it-like-I-see-it tone. Evidently Megan has formed her own unique theory as to what I'm doing. Those chef-types. They think all food is about relationships.

"Her roommate is dating my brother," I say, as

if that somehow fixes things. "Okay, this is a La Marzocco espresso machine. Cream of the crop. It has double independent boilers, which make for consistency from drink to drink. No other machine has that. It's worth it, for a lot of technical reasons I'll get into if you want, but we're here for the taste, right?" To punctuate my point, I shoot off a burst of steam to clear the steam wand. "That's called bleeding the wand and it's important."

"It's all important to you, isn't it?" Suddenly, the restaurant sound system kicks on and Harry Connick, Jr. croons "It Had to be You" from the dining room behind us. Megan's got it coming.

"You betcha," I answer, ignoring Connick's silky voice. "This is the grinder. You always grind to order because this stuff is ground so fine it has a shelf life of two seconds." I grab the porta-filter—the little handled thing that holds the coffee. It's the thing you always see baristas banging to get the old espresso puck (yes, it's called a puck) out.

"Do you make the coffee at your house?" Will asks as I do aforementioned banging. "When your family gets together—do you insist on making the coffee?"

"What do *you* think?" I kick on the grinder, reveling in the aroma. I drove clear across town this morning to get the beans I'm using. Top-notch stuff. The smell of freshly ground espresso—especially espresso this good—is heady perfume to me.

"I have no doubt you're a tyrant at the percolator," he pronounces.

I peer over the machine and laugh. "My dad actually makes a decent cup. My brothers should be banned from the kitchen permanently." I tamp down the grounds, pressing them into the porta-filter. Thirty pounds of even pressure achieving a smooth, uniform surface. That's part of the art of this, but I'll leave that out of Will's little tutorial for the moment. "I do make the coffee. And I bring my own blend. It gets me out of having to bring a side dish, anyway." I run a couple of seconds of water through the machine to ensure Will gets a pristine brew, and place his cup under the spout.

"You're not a cook?"

Tell me, do you readily admit something like this to a man? That you can brew the best coffee on the planet but roasting a chicken eludes you? I hedge. "I can handle the basics. But I'm not in the habit of throwing dinner parties, let's just say that." Harry breaks into yet another crooning ballad behind us, and I decide Megan is purposely meddling. "My sister Cathy? She got Mom's skill in the kitchen. I got my Dad's artistic tendencies." I lock the porta-filter handle into position and push Start. Come on, baby, brew me a twenty-five-second masterpiece.

"I can see that. What is your father's art?"

I pull Will's drink and set it in front of him. "Don't wait. You need to drink it right away." I sit down opposite him while "Unforgettable" wafts through the air.

Will picks up the espresso, staring at the brew. "It's less than two inches deep and I can't see the bottom."

"It's a beverage, Will, not a pond."

He lifts the small cup and tastes it. His eyes close in contemplation. I hold my breath.

"Strong. Sharp." He shakes his head as if to clear it. "It'd wake the dead." His voice has a bit of frog in it, like he's trying to hide his dislike. "I suppose it has its fans on pure strength alone."

I'm disappointed, but not surprised. I'd be astounded if someone who didn't care for coffee liked espresso. It'd be like putting a straw in a can of Hershey Syrup and handing it to someone who didn't like chocolate. "It's an acquired taste, I assure you, but it would be hideous done on a poor machine. You can actually regulate the sweet-sharp component by how you time the pull. On a *quality* machine, that is." My adrenaline kicks into high gear and I pop up back toward the machine. "Let's try the cappuccino. I'm thinking that will be your favorite."

I shoot another blast out of the steam wand just to make sure everything's perfect. "My Dad sculpts," I say, pouring the milk into the small silver steaming pitcher. "Or, he used to sculpt. All the time before we were born, Mom says. Now I'm steaming milk for the cappuccino, which is one-third espresso, one-third steamed milk, and one-third foam." The rich, sweet scent of hot milk rises up.

"Your Dad doesn't sculpt any more?"

"He and mom got married," I say, over the noise of the steamer—which isn't much noise at all when you do it right, by the way. Don't let any second-rate barista fool you into thinking lots of noise makes for good cappuccino. "Then came kids and bills and, well, life took over, as he puts it."

Will frowns and leans back in his chair. "You don't approve?"

"It's as if a part of him's been cut off." I grind and pull another shot of espresso for Will's drink, loving how the sharp coffee aroma blends with the mellow fragrance of the steamed milk. It's such a perfect harmony. "He's a whole man, but there's a passion missing. Hidden. Ignored so long I don't think even he realizes he misses it. But I see it sometimes, when we pass art or sculptures. I can feel some part of him grasping for it. But then he shuts it down."

Will fiddles with the teaspoon at his table. "It's not wrong for a man to do what he needs to in order to take care of the family he loves." His tone makes me look up from pouring the milk into his cup. Will's words have the weight of a sad past pulling on them.

"But God gave my dad a passion and a talent. I don't think Dad had to give that up completely because of us. I don't want that burden. I want him to be happy." I check the foam for perfection and place the cup on the table beside the espresso. "Drink." I want him to like it. I need him to like it.

He studies it for a moment, appreciating the design, noticing how the foam doesn't melt with time, but stands in its own glory. I sit down, watching him sip and my heart slams around in my chest while Connick finally does an upbeat number.

"Different. Mellower, but still with a bite."

"It'd be all bite without a decent machine. Take another sip."

He does. There's the tiniest bit of foam on his lip. I squelch the urge to reach out and wipe it off, pointing awkwardly to my own lip instead to cue him.

"What?" he asks. Then he says, "oh, well, that's an unfortunate side effect," when he understands. He clears his throat and wipes it off.

"Cappuccino's got more character than the straight-shot dump-caffeine-into-my-bloodstream espresso. Feel that smoothness? The firm but silky texture of the foam? That's what a good machine can do."

"You're sure it's not all in the…what's the term? Barista?"

He takes another sip and I take that as a compliment. "Well, sure, it has lots to do with the barista. I can coax a good drink out of a mediocre machine. But I can coax *art* out of this baby." I cast my glance back over her gleaming panels, appreciating her like a gearhead appreciates a sports car. "And the real coffee addicts? The one's who know their stuff? They know that machine on sight. If they see one of those behind the counter, they know they're going to have a fine drink. It's practically its own advertisement."

"It's practically its own mortgage," Will counters. He holds up one hand. "Yes, I admit it does a good job. And," he adds, drawing it out for suspense, "I don't hate it."

I beam. Victory.

"But it is not my drink of choice. I'll admit to having my horizons expanded a bit, but I did not just drink a fourteen-thousand-dollar cup of coffee. I'm still not convinced."

I take a breath to start in on a good rebuttal.

"Entirely," he adds, before I can launch my tirade. He takes a fourth sip. A fourth sip! One sip is obligation. Two sips is good manners, but four sips? That's enjoyment. "You don't think your father is happy?" Will asks as he puts the cup down.

"No, he's happy. It's just that, well, there's *more.* There's more and it would be worth the risk to reach for it." Okay people, we can stop talking about my father now and focus on the coffee. I stand back up. "Now let's have a latte. Americans like to give this one all the bells and whistles."

"Don't you think that's your father's choice? To give up pursuing the art so he can provide for his family?"

"It is. But it's not my choice." I set about pulling the latte.

"Risk has consequences," Will points out. "People get hurt."

"Risk has rewards. God still asks us to risk. Life asks us to risk. Real life, that is, not just a safe version of life." I finish putting the foamy milk mixture in his cup, giving it my signature swirl design. Gorgeous.

Will considers the design when I place it before him. "Impressive."

I sit back down. "All really great baristas have their own signature design."

"Is Higher Grounds your risk?" He returns to our conversation while he lifts the cup.

I've never had anyone put it quite that way before. "I believe it's a great gift to know what you want to risk in life. I think that's where God shows up and surprises us beyond our imaginations. I think stepping beyond our comfort zone is, well, it's one of the most important things we can do in life." I stop talking and wait for his response.

"So this is a latte," he says after a swallow or two. Ugh. He says it in the same way you'd say someone's date was "nice." Definitely not a rave. I launch into a listing of the latte's finer qualities, how it can be made in a variety of ways in dozens of flavors.

Will stops me. "If I want dozens of flavors, I'll go get some ice cream."

"No, really. People love all these flavors."

"Women love all these flavors," Will revises my theory. "When's the last time a strapping young man came into Carter's and ordered a raspberry white chocolate latte?"

Ha. I got him now. "Wednesday." I smirk.

"Who *wasn't* ordering for his girlfriend?"

Rats. Why is it always the tiny details that do you in? "Okay, you may have a point there, but half my customer base is bound to be female."

"But I am not."

Trust me, there's precious little chance of my

forgetting how male William Grey is. "The latte," I say while gesturing for him to take another sip, "is all about the combination. Too much milk and it tastes like a kiddy drink. Not enough, and it's too biting. So?"

His eyes narrow in thought. "It tastes like that high tea you took me to the other day. A lot of window dressing around a middling product."

I cross my arms. "Are you calling my latte *middling?*"

"I'm saying I don't care for it. Not that it's a bad product. I told you I'd give you my honest appraisal, and that's what you're getting."

"You'd be getting a lot less drink on a *middling* machine." I make the word *middling* as whiny as I can. I stare at him. He stares back. "Great," I finally exclaim, throwing my hands up. "You're not convinced. I go through all this trouble—did you know there are people who would kill to get three drinks from a machine like this? Do you have any idea how fabulous these drinks are?"

"No," he says, smiling in the most irritating way, "because *I prefer tea.*"

"Well," I snatch back the espresso, downing the contents because it would be a crime to let such liquid gold to go waste. "Why don't you take your tea-hyping, limey hat off and think like a banker. Like a coffee-loving banker. Like a man who sees the value in excellent equipment to produce a superior product."

"Couldn't you achieve superiority in beans for a

far smaller cash outlay?" Will puts down the latte with the same expression my nephew Charlie gives to his broccoli.

Supremely irritated, I snatch that back, throw an extra dollop of foam on it and down it. It's a stunning latte. Balanced to perfection. The Bible verse about "pearls before swine" jingles through my head. "It's about both. I can't just take a batch of fabulous beans and throw them through your great-aunt Matilda's percolator and make what people want."

Will makes for the cappuccino before I can get my hands on it. "My great-aunt Lydia drank *tea.*"

I snatch that drink out of his unappreciative hands, too. "Well, jolly good for her," I bark as I head back to the machine.

Will gets up and follows me.

I glare at him. "You don't like it. You won't go for the good machines, will you?"

"Do you always assume you know what I think?"

"Isn't it obvious?"

"Well," he says, "I was *going* to say I have a compromise to propose. However, I don't think it qualifies as a compromise when one party hates the idea."

If he won't spring for the La Marzoccos, how much worse can it get? I start shutting the beautiful, unappreciated machine down. "Hate it, will I? Now's who's assuming?"

"Oh, I rather have a feeling you will." There is an unveiled challenge in his eyes.

I settle onto one hip, pitcher still in one hand. "Try me."

"If you want to spend this much on equipment and push your budget up that high, then I'm going to recommend that you get your parents to cosign on the loan."

Kick me next time I say something like "How much worse can it get?" Kick me hard.

"My parents? Were you listening to me just now at all?"

"You're smart, you're talented, but you're not exactly loaded with collateral for a loan that large. It would lower the risk for you. I do believe it's the best way."

"What about rich Uncle Ian?" I say, clutching the dials of this machine now slipping out of my reach. There's got to be another way.

"He's already the source of over half your capital. If you want to ask for all that money, you need your parents."

I slump against the counter. "Well, you're right, I don't like it. As a matter of fact, I hate it." Will says nothing. He's right: this isn't compromise. It's extortion. "You're just joking, right?"

He shakes his head.

I sigh. I knew Higher Grounds was going to cost me, but I didn't count on it costing me my pride. The absolute last *last* thing I wanted was to have to get my parents' help on this. Higher Grounds is my flag of independence. My baby. I would have refused their help if they offered it. But believe me, they're not going to offer it. Dad'll be against this in spades. Mom will be too worried to talk him into it. I'm thinking it would be easier to get Will to down six more cups of coffee than to get them to back my shop.

Talk about your God-sized problems. This is huge.

"I know it's not how you pictured things, so why don't you think this over? Pray about it?" Will says.

I whack the coffee puck out of the porta-filter with more force than is perhaps necessary. "I don't want to think it over. I don't need to think it over. I want these machines. Higher Grounds needs these machines. If that's what it takes to get them, then—" I try not to grind it out through my teeth "—that's what we'll have to do."

Will looks startled. "We?"

"You don't think I can convince them on my own do you? I need the bank to back me up on this. And you're the bank. So back me up."

"And if they say no you'll consider less-expensive machines?"

"Oh, they'll say no. The *first* time I ask them. Which is why I hope you like pot roast, because it's going to take a slew of family dinners to make this happen."

"Pot roast?" Will gulps out.

I hand him the bag of coffee beans I brought with me. "Fire up your British charm, William Grey III, we've got a loud Irish family to win over."

"I'm quite sure I never agreed to this when I said you could show me these machines."

* * *

That man sends my brain into a nonfunctional overdrive.

Do you know how I know? For starters, I invited Will Grey to have dinner with my family. Repeatedly.

I also know because it's now three o'clock in the morning, I'm wide awake and I'm only just *now* realizing that I downed the equivalent of three shots of espresso.

Chapter Twenty

Testing theories

"I can't do this."

I'm staring at my parents' front door from Will's car.

This suddenly seems like a horrendous idea. And this is only the beginning. Tonight is supposed to be getting them just used to the idea of Higher Grounds. Wait till we get to the money part. I'll be heading to China to put the Pacific Ocean between me and *my* dad.

"Come now, everyone gets a little nutters about their family."

I look at him. I've got to tell him now, before we go in the door. I'm an idiot for not fessing up to this earlier, but there's no helping that now. "Will, they don't know about Higher Grounds. Not at all. We're starting from square one here. So be really, really charming."

He runs his hands nervously through this hair. "Nothing? You've told them nothing at all? Just a little awkward, wouldn't you say, Miss Black? How are you going to explain my presence as your loan officer if they don't even know you're thinking about opening a business?"

I just ignore that, because nothing can come from getting into that right now. "I'm punting, okay? Now, remember, no politics, no religion, no finance yet. I'll bring up Higher Grounds when I think they're ready. Oh, and stay away from art and baseball, too. And don't get into music with my brother John, or he'll never stop talking...and..."

Will puts a finger over my mouth, puts his hand on the top of my head and murmurs something.

I look at him, slightly puzzled.

"I believe prayer may be our only hope this evening. I just asked God to bless you."

My heart does a tiny, blessed, somersault.

I stick both my hands on top of his head. "The Lord bless you and keep you, Will Grey." I open one eye and look at him. "'Cause you are *so* gonna need it." I open the door latch. "Let's go."

"No, you don't!" Will reaches across and keeps me from opening the door. He smiles at me and the tiny blessed somersault becomes a triple backflip. "A proper English banker always opens the door for his client."

* * *

"So *you* banged up my baby's nose in the park?" my dad asks as he shakes Will's hand in the foyer.

"Not exactly," Will replies smoothly. "A teammate did the damage. I just served as the rescue squad."

"And I'm *fine,* aren't I, Dad?" I pull Will into the living room where the rest of the family is waiting.

Will whistles softly when he sees most of the Black clan gathered one room. "Look at all that ginger hair."

"Ginger hair?" my brother John says, hoisting a curly-spiky lock of his wild teenage hairstyle. "You mean red hair?"

Will laughs a bit. "Yes. We call it ginger hair."

"Sounds nicer," my sister Cathy chimes in.

John shoots her a look. "Well, if you're a *girl...*"

Suddenly a tumble of ginger-haired children—Cathy's kids tangled in with my brother Steve's two girls—roll in from the den. "Well, hullo, you." Will crouches down until he's eye-to-eye with Charlie, who stares at Will.

"How come you talk funny?"

"I'm British. Like...um...Winnie the Pooh and Christopher Robin."

That seems to be explanation enough for Charlie. "Okay."

"Like Mary Poppins?" my niece Abby calls out.

"Exactly." Will says. "You have ginger hair. I talk funny. We'll get along just fine, if you ask me."

Abby looks like she's about to question that particular theory for a moment, then decides it will work for her. "Yep. Okay." Charlie then pokes her in the ginger hair, and the quartet of cousins tumbles off into the den again, screeching. Followed by Brewster, our huge golden retriever.

"Even the dog is ginger-haired in this house." I laugh. "Come on, you need to meet Mom."

"Well, that failed to work. I tried to steer the conversation toward Higher Grounds three times and each time you stymied it." Will is pulling a large clump of ginger dog hair off his pant leg as he walks up the little patio that leads to my apartment door.

"Stymied?" That man has the oddest choice of verbs.

"Would you prefer I say *chickened out?*"

Ouch. He's right though, that's exactly what I did. I chickened out. Three times. I just can't bring myself to even talk about Higher Grounds, let alone ask them to cosign my loan. "I'm working up to it, okay? I need a little more time."

Will stuffs his hands in his pockets. "You haven't got loads of time, Maggie. Besides, a few more dinners of that size and I'll rival Art in weight and end up a forward on the team."

"Okay, okay, point taken. Can we leave it rest now?" I lean back against the patio railing, taking in the weather. We've had extraordinary weather for Seattle this fall. It's one of those sparkling October nights where the rain has held off and the air is an energizing cool that begs you to pull on a sweater and go take a walk. The street is bustling with people taking in the beauty of the night. Seattle didn't get its reputation for rain out of nowhere—we cherish our nice weather here because we don't have a lot of it to enjoy.

Spanish guitar music lilts out over the dusk from the record store down the street. A spicy smell tells me the Mexican restaurant must be crowded tonight. Again, I'm reminded of why I cherish the colliding textures of my neighborhood. As if to prove my point, a wildly dressed teenager in striped leggings on a unicycle rides up the street, singing at the top of his lungs. Will shakes his head. "You live in a crazy neighborhood."

I nudge him. "I love Fremont. The color, the sounds, everything. Walking to work here is entertainment, not endurance. There's always something weird and wonderful to see. I mean, come on—we even have our own troll."

Will shakes his head. "Oh, that's right. I've heard of it."

"You've seen the troll, haven't you?"

"Only in pictures."

I push myself up off the railing. "Oh, well, we gotta fix that. You need to see the troll. It's only a few blocks from here. Come on. It's the absolute perfect night for it and you can walk off some of that meal. How can you miss the chance to tell the folks back home you've seen the famous Fremont Troll?"

Will gets out his car keys. "I think the folks back

home can survive without a mesmerizing account of the famous Fremont Troll."

"Nope." With a quick move born of countless family squabbles, I snatch Will's car keys out of his hands. "I'd never forgive myself. Anglo-American relations and all." I begin walking toward the bridge where our troll resides. He's not real, our troll, but I imagine you caught on to that. He's a giant, playful, concrete sculpture under the Aurora Avenue bridge. You'll find him in every guidebook and I just adore him. "Do you have any idea," I say to Will as I dangle his car keys just out of reach (which means I'm practically running to stay ahead of him), "how ridiculous you sound saying the folks back home? Try saying y'all come back now, y'hear?"

"Absolutely not." Will lunges for his keys, but a quick pass behind my back—along with a bit of bobbing and weaving—keeps them out of reach. "You're nutters," he says, lunging again, "You know that?"

"Part of my sales and marketing strengths." He's not really trying to best me, you know. The guy plays rugby; he could pick me up and shake the keys out of me if he really wanted to. But there's something so wonderful about this side of him. Feeling bolder, I scoot behind him and cover his eyes. "Oops, stop here." I turn him around the corner so he's facing up the hill toward our famous under-bridge dweller.

"Will you look at that?" Will says under his breath when I uncover his eyes.

"You can climb on him. Come on." Now, I haven't climbed the troll in a good five years, but tonight I find it irresistible. I dash up the hill toward the sculpture. Will hesitates for a moment, shaking his head, then he starts up the street after me. Within minutes we're scrambling over the troll like kids—exploring his head, eyes, nose, hair and the huge hand that clutches a life-size VW Beetle.

By the end of our juvenile adventures we're breathless and silly. Panting, we collapse onto the massive wrist, staring down the bridge pylons and listening to the rhythmic hum of the cars going over the bridge above us. The evening has darkened to a sapphire blue, the lights of Fremont and the draw-bridge over the bay twinkle like a mirror of the star-filled sky. If I had to brew up the perfect fall evening, it would look like this.

"Dinner was…rather wonderful," Will says after a comfortable silence.

"Really?" I blink at him skeptically. "I counted seven different arguments. Were you in the same room with me?"

"How do you do that? How did you learn?" Will leans back on his hands to look at me. A pair of young parents to our left pry their crying child off the troll's hair, telling him it's past his bedtime and it's time to go home.

"Learn what?" I blow an unruly curl out of my eye, laughing at the child because I don't want the night to end, either.

"To argue with all that noise but all that…love."

"You're talking about *my* family? The sixteen-person riot we just had dinner with? Are you *sure* you were in the same room with me?"

"I don't see how you can do that," Will says, his voice full of amazement. "You all never stopped arguing with each other all night but I never for a single moment felt anything but affection. How… how do you all do that?"

I realize, with a tender sting of pity, that I don't know how I could ever explain such a thing. I've known that loud kind of love since my first breath. It would be like explaining breathing—it just happens, you don't try to make it happen. "I don't know," I finally reply with a quiet voice, kicking at the gravel around my feet. "It's just how we love each other, I suppose. It's how it's always been."

Will falls silent. I stare at him, his face shadowed in the dappled light streaming though the bridge. Over our heads, the rhythmic thumping hum of passing cars feels like the troll's giant heartbeat. I know, without his saying a word, that it's how it's *never* been for him. I know, even though he's right next to me, that his thoughts are halfway around the world and a dozen years in the past.

I look at him, see the furrow in his brow and the tight angle of his mouth. I wonder, suddenly, if he looks like his father.

It was at that moment that I became the bravest of all. "You need to forgive him someday, Will. Maybe that's why you're here. Why you've met my family. God knows how much you've hurt over this for all these years. Maybe God wants you to realize that the hurt will never go away until you can forgive him for being who he is."

A long time and several deep breaths pass before his reply. "Why is it you are always going places I'm trying not to bring you?" There is both pain and thankfulness in his voice. Slowly, his hand comes across the concrete to rest quietly next to mine.

We have touched before, Will and I. Minutes, hours, days and weeks ago. But tonight, as our hands sit touching side by side, it feels altogether new and different.

When he turns to me, his eyes rival the night sky. "There's something I should have done a long time ago. Are you free Tuesday night?"

Chapter Twenty-One

Not even in sonnet form

Saturday morning, Diane dumps half a cup of cream into her mug. The woman puts so much cream and sugar into her coffee it's hard to even call it coffee anymore. "So." She plunks herself down backward in a kitchen chair, staring at me with inquiring eyes after I've told her the entire coffee-tasting and dinner-eating story. "You chickened out. Will's right, you know, you should tell your family. I mean, if not now, when?"

I evade the question. "He invited me to tea. I don't know if it's a date or a beverage rebuttal to my coffee demonstration, but I'm supposed to meet him at The House of Blue Leaves on Tuesday." I pour my own cup. Yes, that's right, tea. Hey, look, if you'd have seen the way he looked at me when he said it, you had said yes to anything. He could have asked me to a beef-jerky tasting and I'd have consented.

"Do I get to voice my concerns here? I know what I said earlier, but I thought you guys were going to be more careful, not spend more time together. Are you sure you know what you're doing? Why are you having tea with your banker Tuesday night?"

"Because I want to."

"Fine. Be that way. Go for the supremely complicated relationship. Me? I've changed my mind. I think you should go with Nate. He likes coffee. He understands coffee. He doesn't hold your credit rating in his tight British fists. Date Nate. Hey, that rhymes."

I glare at Diane. "No. I will not date Nate, even if it rhymes. Not even if you put it in sonnet form. He's a nice guy but it's purely friendship. *Friend*ship. You can have male friends, Diane. You are aware of that option?"

"I'm just saying he could be more than just a friend."

"No," I say firmly. "Friend. Friend only. There's no *zing* there, not even a shred."

Diane takes a deep drink of coffee and starts rooting through the tin of cookies Mom sent home with me last night. As if I don't already spend my days surrounded by baked goods at Carter's. "Does there have to be zing right away? Working up to zing is good. Probably smart. Instant zing gets lots of people into trouble."

"Can we please drop the subject?" I moan, refilling my mug.

Diane doesn't actually drop the subject, just twists it around a bit. She's good at that. "You didn't really get him to do the whipped cream thing, did you?"

"I most certainly did," I reply, snagging my favorite type of cookie out of the tin. "He was fabulous at it. The way his Brazilian accent sounds saying whipped cream should be illegal. The woman practically walked out of the store on air." I chuckle. "Renato," I say, rolling the R for effect, "has a new secret weapon and, trust me, he's not afraid to use it."

Diane eyes me over her cookie. "When's your shift today?"

"Two to ten." I pop a second cookie into my mouth. "Why?"

"I think I should drop by and test the theory."

I glare at her, stifling a giggle. "You wouldn't. I couldn't keep a straight face."

"I would," Diane confirms. "And I will." She shoots up off the chair with new enthusiasm. "Gotta go. Thanks for the coffee and—" she points at me "—I'll see you and your whip-cream-toting friend later."

You know, I was thinking work today was going to be boring. I doubt that'll be the case now.

Downtown, the Saturday afternoon-evening shift at Carter's is always kind of dry. It picks up just around eight, but in the early afternoon there isn't a lot of business in a downtown location. I'll have to remember to add some kind of entertainment, book signings or something, to bring in the Saturday-afternoon crowd to my place. Maybe even a children's story hour. With extra whipped cream on every hot chocolate.

Speaking of whipped cream, I hope Nate hasn't noticed me keeping an eye on the door all day. It's three-thirty now and I've been working since two. And every time a female walks through the door my pulse skips. I don't know how I'm going to keep from laughing when Diane walks in. I'm pretty sure Nate won't recognize her—Diane usually meets me outside.

4:06 p.m., the door swings open. It's Diane. She's put on what I secretly know to be her "extra cute" outfit. She's carrying two shopping bags, but if I know Diane they're just stuffed with empty boxes for effect. Diane is the only ex-theater-major nurse I've ever met. It makes for an odd combination, but I've seen her do funny voices to calm down hurt kids so God must have known what He was doing.

Right now, she's playing the part to the hilt. It's killing me to keep a straight face. I feel a giggle coming on, so I purposely spill a handful of coffee beans on the floor. It gives me a chance to look down and forces Nate to pull her drink.

"What'll it be?" Nate has his smooth voice on. I turn away and roll my eyes.

"Tall hazelnut latte please. Skim milk."

Here it comes. I cough, just to keep the laughs at bay.

"You want whipped cream on that?"

"Ooo," Diane coos, "maybe just a smidge."

You know, there are days where I love this job. I keep my head down, because my face is contorted from suppressing a laugh. I hear the steam go, hear the milk pour and see him reach down into the fridge for the whipped cream canister. Ten, nine, eight, seven…

"Whoa!" From my hiding spot under the counter I hear the sound of rampant dairy product. "That's a bit more than you asked for. I could pull another drink for you, if you want…" That man's voice hints at everything when he says it like that.

"Oh, no, that's okay." I can hear the laugh tickling the edges of Diane's voice. Nate probably thinks she's flirting. This is Diane we're talking about. I'm not sure she knows any other way to talk to a guy. God needs to send that woman a husband, pronto. Her biological clock isn't just ticking, it's registering on the Richter scale.

I've resorted to picking up the coffee beans one by one just to buy myself some time because if I stand up now, I'll blow the whole covert operation. Nate and Diane make small talk for a few minutes while I invent reasons to stay down behind the counter. Finally, I hear the door close behind Diane and I pull in a deep breath. That was just too much fun.

Suddenly I feel Nate squat down beside me. "You got any more tricks like that up your sleeve? That thing works wonders."

Chapter Twenty-Two

The agony and the ecstasy

Funky—elegant. That's how I'd describe this place. The House of Blue Leaves is amazing. I don't know how Will found it, but this is the teahouse I'd open if I ever opened a teahouse. Hip. Sophisticated in a clean-lined, Oriental style but with a dash of artistic flair. The decor is a combination of light wood and black lacquer. Intricate Japanese silk prints hang beside bright red ceramic sconces. A huge Chinese-dragon kite circles around the iron fireplace in the corner. Fascinatingly foreign music wafts underneath the animated conversation going on at a dozen or so intimate tables.

Behind the red-tiled counter, the wild pottery vase doesn't look odd next to the delicate porcelain cups—somehow they go together.

"Hello, William" a man in a black Chinese jacket greets us, bowing three times.

Will bows back. "Hello, Longwei. This is Maggie. I'm teaching her about estate teas tonight."

"Ah. Very good." Longwei hands Will the equivalent of a wine list. I watch Will scan it, running one finger down the list until it stops at something with a price tag higher than the last really good dinner I had. Tea gets that expensive? Tea gets this complicated?

"*Kung Fu Cha,* please. The *Pur-eh* tea. I see you have the 1996 *Mengahai Beeng Cha* on this list," Will says, the Chinese rolling off his tongue with astounding ease. "Have you got 1992 by any chance?"

The server smiles, impressed. I have to say, I'm impressed.

"We keep that in the back."

"We'll have that, *M goi nei sin.*"

"This way, please, and I'll get it ready." All he did was order tea, right? I know he just ordered an impressive kind of tea, but for all I know he could have just asked Longwei to bring us fuchsia rain boots with a side of caviar.

"You speak Chinese?" I gasp as we settle into a little corner alcove behind a white paper screen. A table and two crimson cushions are artfully arranged so that we have privacy but can still see the room around the fire. The corner booth is one thing. But our own little teahouse? How much cooler is that?

I have to admit, I love this place. The clientele is

all across the board: tattooed biker couples in booths next to organic-intellectual types. Artistic black-clad poet-types next to upscale executives. Elderly Chinese couples next to two women laden with shopping bags. Every ethnicity, every social status, casual drinkers and people who seem to really know their stuff. No one would ever feel out of place here. The crowd is the very definition of the word *eclectic*.

"I spent a year in Hong Kong when I was young. One of—" he hesitates a second "—my father's many adventures. I couldn't negotiate a peace treaty, but I can hold my own in a restaurant. When your boss in the flower shop laid into Art on your behalf, I'm afraid I understood most of what she said. I might have gotten the rest if she had slowed down a bit, but what I did hear was already burning my ears off."

I can only imagine. Nancy's told me off in English more than once and I can guess how much more apt she is in her mother tongue.

This is so far from the ruffle-laden tea stunt I put him through, I can't even begin to make up for my bad behavior. I admire the elegant flower arrangement on our table. "This place is absolutely amazing."

"And, I might add, not a speck of chintz in sight. Sometimes the American version of high tea just makes me laugh. It's as though you've created a tea theme-park ride. All fluff and doilies and bitty sandwiches."

"Yeah." I wince. "Sorry about that. But you handled it really well."

"You're not the first to try that, you know. I'm forever telling people that most British don't do high tea the way you all think we do. Actually, a British tea is much closer to the Asian tea concept than to *Mary Poppins* or *Alice in Wonderland*." Will gestures around the room. "I think this place does an excellent job. On Saturdays they have live music—everything from jazz guitars to classical sitar. It's become rather a favorite of mine—I hope you can see why."

Longwei slides back the screen and presents us with a mini-brazier, setting it carefully in the center of the table. He places a large iron kettle on the brazier, then bows at each of us. Will lowers his head in reply and I follow his lead. I'd noticed the same kettle on several other tables when we came in.

Me. Looking forward to tea. Could you ever imagine that'd be the case?

"Hot water," Will says after Longwei leaves. "The temperature of the water is absolutely essential to good tea." His voice is formal, but his eyes sparkle. He's enjoying this immensely. He pushes up the sleeves of his shirt, flexing his fingers in readiness. "The point of all this is to achieve excellence. To create superior tea. Under superior circumstances. Surely you can appreciate that."

I can. I do. The water's not even hot yet and I'm enjoying myself immensely. What if I hate the tea? I mean, I don't much care for tea under mediocre circumstances. What if he goes through all this and

I still hate it? Deceptive or not, I'd probably fake it just to keep that look on his face.

Longwei returns, bearing a slotted wooden tray filled with all kinds of objects: a small, squat teapot and matching pitcher, half a dozen assorted china cups and bowls in different sizes and shapes, a wooden container of odd-looking tools and a dish of something black and crinkly that I think is the tea but looks like a freeze-dried shrub.

"Now, as I said, temperature is the key. So we heat up the pot." Will pours water from the now-hissing kettle into the teapot and keeps pouring.

"It's going to run over," I say, reaching to stop his hand.

"It's supposed to run over. That's part of the ritual. It's a symbol of abundance. 'My cup runneth over' and all. The box is designed to hold the extra water. This way every inch of the pot is heated and cleaned."

It sounds Zen, but he just quoted a Bible verse. My head is spinning—and you know, I've decided that's not all bad.

Will pours the water from the pot into one set of bowls, then another. "The cups come next. Inside and out, like the pot." He pours the water over the cups, then uses the wooden tongs to dip the cups into each other, heating the outside. Concentrating, but glancing up every now and then with a dashing look in his eyes. "When I'm all done, you'll never look at a teabag in the same way again." The man is fired up, ready to change my mind.

"You never want to touch the tea with your hands." He loads the tea into the center of the pot with a wooden implement. "And you never want to shock it, so you pour carefully." He pours the water around the pile of tea, then raises and lowers the pot three times while he finishes pouring. "It's like the bow. Three times for respect. But we don't drink this one. It's called the foot water, and it's mostly to wash the tea and get it ready." He does the whole thing again, slips the lid on and lets it steep for a few seconds. Then, his eyes widening, he picks up the lid. "Now look." I lean in to see inside the pot and he leans in as well. We're so close to each other I can feel his hair brush my tumbling curls. "It unfurls." He almost whispers and I feel the word *unfurl* in my stomach. Slowly, gracefully, the leaves emerge from their crumpled pellets. "They call it the agony of the tea," Will says as if revealing a secret, "but I've never quite seen it that way." The heady scent of the tea, the nearness of this extraordinary, surprising man—it's so much to take in.

For the next hour, Will goes through a complicated, almost choreographed ritual of pouring and serving this extraordinary thing called tea. Wow. I couldn't have been more wrong about this. It's nothing short of chivalrous and it's the furthest thing from sissy I can imagine. It's like, well, the Kung Fu name makes sense now: it's like a martial art. Clean and solid with a sense of purpose so sharp it takes your breath away.

He explains each step in exquisite detail, catching my eye every now and then. After all the preparation, the single act of him handing me a cup of tea—the way he looked at me, the way he placed it in my hands, the way our fingers touched for far longer than they needed to—it all made my head spin.

The most astounding thing was that when I stole a look around the room, I saw the same thing going on at table after table: dreamy-eyed women accepting cups of tea from men of every shape and size. Even the biker dude had his date absolutely smitten over teensy china cups. I wouldn't have believed it if I hadn't seen it with my own eyes.

"Well?" Will inquires after we finish the first cup (he tells me the ritual involves three cups—oh, boy), "What do you think?"

What do I think? I'm having trouble thinking clearly at the moment, that's what I think.

"I'm surprised," I reply, because it's true. Is it my new favorite drink? No. Do I care right now? No. Will I stick around for two more cups? You betcha. "The tea's okay, but it's about so much more than just the tea." *Oh, Maggie, is that the best you could come up with? Even Diane would groan at that one and she'll fall for any line.* "I can see why wome—people like it."

Will stares for a moment. "You'd be mobbed in Hong Kong, you know."

"Really?" I reply. "Brutal to coffee-lovers over there, are they?"

"No." Will laughs, shaking his head as he puts his tea cup back onto the ornate wooden tray. "The ginger hair. You hardly ever see that color over there. You'd stand out like a torchlight."

"The ginger-haired woman," I say, feeling an urge to toss my hair, "I like the sound of that. Sounds like an epic novel. Much better than redhead."

Will leans on his elbow. The light green shirt he has on makes his eyes come alive. "I've never seen a family of all ginger. Do you get lots of stares when you go out?"

"I don't know. I never even think about it. Dad and Mom, of course, are more gray than red now. Even when she started to go really gray, Mom wouldn't dye her hair. She said no one ever got it right except for God when it came to red hair."

Will nods over toward the biker couple—more specifically, toward the candy-apple-red hair of the woman in the pair. "I'd have to say I agree with your mom on that one."

"It has it's downsides. Any Irishman will tell you that the fiery hair comes with a fiery temper."

"Oh," Will replies, "I think I can attest to that. I have had that fiery temper corner me in the office, remember." He smirks, remembering the scene. "And the rows you all got into that night at your house."

"Rows?" I tease him. "Yeah, we row all right. We give row a bad name."

You can see Will recalling the madness in his head. "I used to imagine having those when I was a kid. You can guess family dinners at my house were a far...quieter affair."

"All one lump or two?" I adopt a pathetic English accent.

"Not quite that bad. But definitely on the stodgy side."

"I don't mind the noise. Dad always said our family was loud with love. My brothers tease me mercilessly, but they'd be there for me in a heartbeat."

"I can see that." Will's voice and his eyes are so far away, I'm reminded again of the differences between our families. We couldn't have come from more contrasting homes. My family is loud, annoying and in my face, but there's so much love behind the commotion. I look at Will's face and I see the reflection of a home that was neat, clean, considerate…and cold. "It's nice," he says softly.

"It is," I say softly, meaning it, "even when it drives you nuts, it's still nice."

There is a long moment of quiet between us. Will pours more tea.

"Maggie, why haven't you been able to tell your family about Higher Grounds? Honestly," Will grins as he toasts me with the last cup, "your large family provides you with a ready-made customer base."

Now whose turn is it to go places I'm not ready to bring him? It takes me a minute to decide how to answer. "Have you ever had something so important to you that you can't bear even the slightest opposition to it? So you keep it close—really close—until you know you're ready? Even if you're not sure you'll ever be ready?"

I think I expected him launch into a speech about how I need my parents' backing. "Maggie Black," he says softly instead, "you continue to surprise me."

"I'm a wimp," I blurt out over my own breathlessness, "what's so surprising about that?"

Will smiles. "Because you seem to me be the kind of person who'd be shouting about Higher Grounds on street corners."

I feel the blood rush up to my face. "Not this." I hadn't even realized until just this moment what a confession that is. I'm suddenly acutely aware—intimately, completely aware—that Will is the only man on Earth who knows my dream.

As if reading my thoughts-or the dumbstruck look that must be on my face-Will leans in and says, "Maggie, how many people know about Higher Grounds?"

I feel like the answer will take us down a path neither of us will be able to stop. Part of me is ready to go there, while another part of me is scared to death. "Not counting class? Me, Diane, God—" I hesitate what feels like two hours before I finish "—and you."

Will stares into my eyes. "I'm honored," he says and the tone of his voice washes over me. Physically. I mean it. A million sensations hit me in those words.

Without meaning to, maybe without even being able to help it, we just crossed a line. *The* line. It's not a line in the sand that corporate policies draw like a touch or a remark. Those are external things. You can go back on those. Apologize for inappropriate banker-client relations and so on.

But us, we can't go back from here. I think we both know it, we can't fool ourselves into thinking we can anymore. I'll never be able to close back up the piece of me that he's opened. He'll always own it. And I know, in a way I can't even begin to explain, that he'll always honor it. Cherish it, even, although that's such a dorky word. My heart does something that I couldn't stop even if I wanted to.

And, for better or worse, I know I don't want to stop it.

Dear Lord, Heavenly Father, I've just fallen for my banker. Hard. What on earth do I do now?

I don't remember how we got out of the teahouse. But when we stood on the riverbank, watching the sun splash a pastel palette on the water, I knew he was wrestling with all of it. And so I cherished it: his honor, his integrity, his caution. I waited for him to turn to me, because I knew he had to be the one to turn first. And because I knew, no matter how long it took, that he would.

When he did, the universe ground to a halt. You read about that stuff, about the whole world boiling down to one moment where your heart spills open. That moment where it's not about how cute he looks or some external attribute but it goes infinitely deeper into something you can't even fit into words. You hope it might happen to you, but there's always some part of you that thinks those things are only for *other* people. Other, worthier, blessed people who have less ordinary lives.

I feel Will's hands wrap themselves around my

shoulders. Slowly, deliberately, like a declaration. "I shouldn't," he whispers.

"I know," I whisper back, barely audible.

His kiss is so tender, so filled with everything it's cost him, that I nearly weep. To be worth that to someone. What more extraordinary thing is there?

I think of the agony of the tea, unfurling into the heat. We share an exquisite moment of unfurling tenderness. Of careful, costly, revelation. Of admitting what we'd both known for weeks. The unbearable bliss of unfolding my heart after a dried and crumpled season.

Who knew love was like tea?

Who knew I was in love?

I am startled and, then again, not surprised at all.

Chapter Twenty-Three

Yikes

"Tea? Just making cups of tea?"

I throw Diane a look. She rang my doorbell at eight-thirty this morning, dying to know how things turned out. I made her coffee while she grilled me for all the details. "It's not so much what's in the cups as how it all flows together."

"Oh, it's flowing together, all right, I can see that. But tea? Sounds weak." She hoists her hand with her little finger extended. "Pinky out and all."

"You wouldn't say that if you saw what I saw last night. Every woman in the place was swooning over the guys who were serving them tea. Not a poking pinky in sight, either, mind you. I tell you, these Chinese are onto something."

"They must be if he kissed you. He *kissed* you, Maggie. Wait, what is the word the British use for it?

I saw it in a movie once… *Snogged.* Maggie Black is snogging her banker. That's front-page news."

"You wouldn't!" I threaten her with a teaspoon.

She smiles. "You know I wouldn't." She puts down her coffee and leans in. "Wow, was it wonderful?"

I'm sure my face just gained two shades of pink. "I think it was ten minutes before I could even breathe." I take a deep breath. "I'm in love with him, Di."

Diane brings her feet up to curl on my couch. "I figured that out two weeks ago." She smiles warmly. "Glad you caught on. So now what?"

I lean back, my hands covering my face. "I don't know. This is so complicated on so many fronts. Bank…family…"

"So what did he say when you told him?"

I wince. "I haven't told him, yet."

She gives me a long look letting me know just what she thinks of the wisdom of my silence.

"Well, I haven't found the right moment. Oh, why did God make romance wacko? First I can't find a decent guy for years, then I fall for the most complicated man and relationship you can imagine." I squint my eyes shut. "God should know better. We're just human. We can't handle anything this complicated."

I feel Diane pat my head in true nurse bedside manner. "This, from a girl who can make twenty-seven different drinks from an ounce of tiny roasted beans."

* * *

"Tonight we're covering personnel issues." Will writes *personnel* on the whiteboard. "That's more of a concern for some of you than for others, but we're also going to talk about the *personal* cost of entrepreneurship." He writes *personal* underneath the first word.

Talk about your touchy subjects. The personal cost? How about my heart? Please tell me he had this on the syllabus before we kissed, that he didn't add it as a response. I'm already feeling weird enough as it is, I don't need to be second-guessing Will's subconscious choice of lesson plans.

"How many of you will have staff from the day you open?"

About half the hands in class go up. Josh, our virtual-billionaire wannabe, if you remember, has his hand resolutely down. No surprise there. And really, would *you* want to work for cyber-guy? After you fit Josh and his whopping ego in his ready-to-launch success-garage, do you think there'd be room for anyone else? On the other hand, it might be entertaining; that man and his ego are their own one-man circus.

"Payroll—and the resulting paperwork, not to mention the costs of salary and benefits, is one of the hardest challenges of a small business. You may love making teddy bears and dream of doing it full-time, but when a huge portion of your daily life is calculating Social Security and writing out dozens of checks, you'll find it loses it's charm. You may find that once you go full-time into the pasta-sauce business," Will says, pointing to Jerry Davis, "you actually spend far less time cooking pasta sauce than you do now." Jerry flinches. "Not that I'm aiming to scare you, but I do want you to understand that the passion that brought you here is going to be doing battle with the realities of business. It's important to understand how much of a business person you want to be on a daily basis. For some of you, the solution to keeping your passion intact is to hire someone else to handle the day-to-day managerial operations."

Josh looks like he considers that a cop-out for the less gifted. Will eyes him. "I can hardly picture you standing in line to refill your postage meter, Mr. Mason."

"I'll do it online, Grey. I'll do everything online."

Will sits down on his desk. Ooo, big point coming. "Including see your doctor, remember your mother's birthday and keep a serious relationship going? Have you given any thought, Mr. Mason, to the health and wellness factors of running an intensive small business? Do you have any idea, for example, the number of marriages that fail to survive the opening of a restaurant? You may, in fact, be matching up lovers at the expense of your own love life. Or how about the number of heart attacks and ulcers suffered by software executives before their first IPO? Those numbers might wake you up faster than Miss Black's darkest espresso."

Josh looks more startled than I do.

"Again, Mr. Mason, I'm not saying your life is about to turn to rubbish. I'm just saying these are things you need to take into consideration before you decide you'll handle it all on your own. It's the most common entrepreneurial mistake—self-sufficiency. You're far better off budgeting for as much outsourcing or staffing as you can handle in the early months. And recognizing that your life is going to be on hold for a while. I'd never advise anyone to start a business and start a family at the same time."

That wasn't directed at me, was it? Will's been looking like he'd swallowed something sour all night. When he handed back my budget worksheet, I got a B- with a Post-it note that said simply My Office After stuck on it, folded under so that only I could see it.

He's changed his mind. He's going to tell me I'll have to take the whole course over again with some other teacher. He'll postpone my loan application. I'm doomed.

No wait, it might not be like that. Will thought long and hard about everything, I know he did. He's the kind of guy who doesn't go back once he's made his mind up about something. Some guys just move out of the house when they fight with their dad, Will crossed an ocean. A little emotional complication isn't going to give him cold feet.

Is it?

I'm not sure I heard a single word the rest of

class. I just kept staring at that Post-it, filled with large, precise letters. It didn't look like a meet-me note, it looked like a warning label.

Oh, Father God, I sure hope You know what You're doing here. You know I love him. I've prayed about this to You so much my head and heart are spinning. I'm trying to trust You, but can I just remind You of my current stress level here?

My nerves are wound tight as I try to give the impression of walking calmly to Will's office. Of course I'm not calm—I'm a wreck—but I can shoot for at least looking calm.

"Come in." He still has his teacher voice on.

"What's going on, Will?"

Will motions for me to sit in the guest chair, then parks his hip on the corner of his desk. That's like sitting on his desk, which can only mean something big is coming. I feel slightly ill. "Um…" Will runs his hands through his hair.

"Will?" I gulp his name out, feeling like a giant hand has just clamped itself around my throat.

"Look, I…the fact of the matter is…there's something I should have told you earlier. Something you should see. It's technically confidential, but in light of…things, I think I'd be making a far greater error by not telling you."

Chapter Twenty-Four

You're telling me

He's married. He's secretly second in line to the throne of England. The bank has announced a ban on further coffee-bar financing. He's James Bond. I have no idea what's coming. The look on his face is unreadable.

"Alex Matthews was sacked yesterday."

Still in the dark. "Sacked? Who's Alex Matthews? And what's that got to do with anything?"

Will pulls a sheet of paper from a file. "Fired. Alex Matthews was one of the other loan officers from this bank. And he was sacked for suspicion of harassment. Sexual harassment. Of a *client*."

"What did he do?"

"I don't know that Alex did anything. That's the worst of it. He's denying everything, but the client is pressing charges. There's doubt on both sides and no one knows who to believe. Alex is a good fellow. He's engaged to be married, even. The bank's simply sacked him under the pressure of the lawsuit."

"They can do that?"

"It's so early no one really knows. Alex is trying to find a good attorney but the damage is done, as you can imagine."

"That's awful."

"It's far more than that."

I'm such an idiot, I don't even put the pieces together until just this second. "Will," I say looking straight at him, "I'm not going to sue you for kissing me. Hey, another six minutes and I would have kissed you first. I came after you, remember?"

Will shoots me a keep-your-voice-down glare. "Things have been boiling up around Alex for weeks. Everyone is very nervous. Now can you at least understand why I've been—" he pinches the bridge of his nose, searching for the right word "—treading so carefully?"

"No one's harassing anybody here. We're both adults. Sure, it's a little nerve-racking, but it's not the end of the world. It doesn't have to affect us."

Will looks straight at me. "It does, Maggie. It already has. This could be the end of your loan."

"Why? How?"

"If we stay…involved…I'm going to have to move your loan to another officer. I can't stay on your file if I'm…emotionally biased."

On some level, I think I knew that. But now, the way Will looks, the way I now feel, it seems the worst of news. "How bad is that? They just put someone else in charge of my application, right?" My words slow down as I say them, the implications of having someone else on my application dawning on me. I could get anyone. I could get someone who won't even give me serious consideration.

"There are—*were* only three loan officers at this bank. Alex, myself and Stephen Markham. Stephen Markham happens to be the last person on earth I'd want to review your loan."

"Oh." Actually, I think that was more of a gulp than a reply.

"Think about it, Maggie. If I have to transfer your loan to another officer because I've got to admit to an emotional attachment to you—and I'll *have* to admit to an emotional attachment to you if we keep on—the bank is going to have fits in light of what's going on with Alex." Will gets up and starts pacing the room. "It was uphill enough if you got Alex, but he was a good fellow. Now, the managers will be all over me given what's happening with Alex and it'll hand Markham every reason to turn down your loan without even reading it. And no one will blink an eye. They'll all be glad to be rid of a sticky wicket. You won't stand a chance."

I stopped paying attention after "if we keep on." If. As in *we might not.* "What do you mean if?" I gasp out.

"If?"

"You said 'if we keep on.' Like there's a chance

we won't. Like you've already decided. It took me eight weeks, hours of prayer, an overdose of caffeine and the biggest risk I can think of to get to on. Now you just switch to if as if it means nothing?"

Will stops pacing. "What did you just say?"

I'm not making any sense, am I? I blow out a breath. "You're saying you want to stop us because it'll mean a risk to the loan."

"I didn't say that."

"Sure you did. You said we'll have to stop seeing each other or else you'll have to drop yourself off my loan."

"I said 'if.' If as in *yet to be determined.* As in we have to talk about what to do."

Talk about what to do? Who's lord hero protective man kidding? I can see it in his eyes—he's already decided what he thinks we should do. He's going to call it off between us so he can get my loan to approval.

Out of nowhere, I hear Diane's words to me a few weeks ago. *What if what God wants for you is to meet Will? Have you ever considered that Higher Grounds might just only be His way of introducing you?*

That puts me in a full-blown panic. "Talk?" I bark back at Will. "You've already made up your mind, haven't you?"

"It's too much of a risk." Will's voice is filled with finality.

"Don't you think that *I* should be the one to decide that?"

Will throws the memo down on his desk. "We *are* talking. But I'm supposed to be advising you. That's my job."

"There's a mile of difference between advising me and telling me what to do. Deciding *for* me." His kiss tilted the world off its axis. Now Will wants to go and pretend nothing happened between us? How could it be so easy for him?

"I'm doing this because I care about what happens to you." He's trying so hard to keep his voice down he's practically grinding the words out through clenched teeth. "Can't you see that?"

"Then care about what happens to *us*. Why on earth would you make me choose between you and Higher Grounds if there was a way I didn't have to? Even if it was a harder way?"

"Hard? You don't stand a chance with Markham."

"You don't know that." I fire back. "I convinced you, didn't I? I'll just find a way to convince this Markham guy."

"Look, we shouldn't see each other while your loan is being processed. But that's not forever. Maybe a few months after your loan is approved…"

I don't want to wait months for this man. It took me long enough to figure out I was in love with him. I'm the least patient person I know—especially once I know what it is I want. And that's the point here, isn't it? What I want? In that moment, with a wash of clarity, I know what I want to do.

"I want to take my chances with Markham. With you."

"Maggie…"

"I know it's risky. But don't you see?" I sit on the edge of his desk, getting as close as I dare under the circumstances. "We can do this. God is probably planning on us doing this. Sure, there are new hurdles, but think of it this way—once you're off my file as my loan officer, you can help me more. Coach me."

"I've already thought about that," Will replies, "Believe me. You're taking an enormous risk here on very slim chances. Of course I'll do everything I can to strengthen your position with Markham. But Maggie, that's going to mean you *must* have your parents on the loan if you're to stand a chance at all." He stares at me with stern, serious eyes. "You must have their support. You've got to get them on board, immediately. There's no other way."

Chapter Twenty-Five

Plan B Cute

Diane and I sort through a pile of men's clothes at church Monday night while trying to sort through my treacherous state of affairs as well.

She holds up a particularly ugly tie—a red and orange number featuring a mariachi band and palm trees. "Ugh. Someone once paid money to own this? And someone else will want it?"

"Hey, teenagers wear them as belts now. The wilder the better. That's the beauty of vintage."

Diane grimaces, holding the tie as if it could contaminate her on contact. "There's vintage and then there's simply used." She drops the offending neckwear into a box. "Hey, speaking of used, how's Cathy's old computer working out for you? Did you get it up and running?"

I put down the corduroy bell-bottom pants (no, not

flare leg, flares are from *this* decade. Bell-bottoms come from a slightly earlier era) I'm folding. "Only after about two hours with Cathy's husband. *Free* isn't free anymore, either. I had to spend about a hundred dollars on cables and adapters and stuff to get it talking to my printer and my Internet connection. But I'm running loads of spiffy new software now, so I can wow the bank with spreadsheets and—" I deepen my voice to sound like a radio announcer "—desktop publishing."

Diane grabs a handful of hangers to start hanging dress shirts. "So how'd Cathy like your idea?"

I'd hide my face behind the pants if they didn't smell so funny. "I didn't tell her. I couldn't get a moment alone with her."

"What? You're ready to tell Cathy but not her husband? I thought you liked Eric."

"I'm going over to her house tomorrow morning before work. I'm going to tell her then. Look, I just need to start with her, alone. I'll need her help when Mom and Dad go berserk when I tell them. I need to gather my troops in phases here."

Finishing the last shirt button, Diane practically slams the shirt onto the closet rod behind her. "Margaret Black. You are the person I know who cares *least* about what other people think. You take risks that would choke other people. What is the problem with telling your own family—those nice people who love you—about your life's vocation? This is *nuts.* I don't get it. And you don't have a whole lot of time, Maggie. You've *got* to do this."

I've only told myself that about four hundred times. "I know, I know." I wince. "I—I just can't. It's like it's too important. If they think it's a dumb idea I don't know what I'll do."

That answer did not satisfy Diane. She's standing over me, looking at me like I just made no sense. Which is sensible, because I didn't make any sense.

"Do *I* think it's a dumb idea?" she asks, threatening me with a tuxedo shirt in a very frightening coral.

"No," I venture, suddenly unsure even though I know the answer.

"Does Will think it's a dumb idea?"

"Risky maybe, but not dumb."

"And even when he wasn't sure about it, you convinced him, right?"

I smirk. "Well, it does seem like there were other factors at play."

"Will Grey is not the type to let a pretty face overthrow his business sense." At which point she nudges me. "Most of the time. So wise up and realize that Cathy and your parents are going to be on your side, okay? I'm pretty sure God is on your side. Everyone wants you to be happy. It's going to be fine."

I cringe, still nervous. "Can I have that in writing?"

"I can do better than that. I'll be praying for you." She closes her eyes, folds her hands and laments, "Father, have mercy on the poor deluded soul of Margaret Mary Black."

I poke her in the arm. "You're nutters. But between

you and Will, there might be enough praying going on to do the trick."

"Nutters?" she teases. "Ooo, British phraseology. Now I know you're in love with the guy. You have finally told him, haven't you?"

"I'm scaling one emotional Everest at a time, thanks. Will's a cautious guy. I don't want to spook him off while everything's so dicey."

Diane makes an exasperated groan. "Hello? Love? Important thing he might want to know? Exciting thing he might feel back? Now look here, you can hedge over the loan stuff, you can stall your own loving family for reasons I'll never understand, but this is important. You love the guy. I'm thinking he loves you. Don't go getting cold feet now—not when it really matters."

"But I'm scared." It pipes out of me in a preschooler's voice.

Diane sighs. "Honey, we're all scared. You just feel it less often than the rest of us. You're the bravest person I know, Mags. This is love and family on the line here. It's the best time of all to be brave."

She was yukking it up at the clothing ministry, but make no mistake—Diane takes her praying very seriously. It's nine-thirty Tuesday morning and you can be sure that woman is praying up a storm on my behalf right this second. And somewhere in Seattle Will Grey is doing the same. The knowledge of those pair of prayer warriors is the only thing keeping my blood pressure down to a dull roar as I sit in Cathy's kitchen and spill my dream.

"So opening that kind of coffeehouse is what I want to do with Uncle Ian's money. Only it isn't enough, so I'm going to have to do some serious financing."

"Well, it does explain the sudden interest in business software. And it certainly explains why you're working for the big bad coffee corporation— I couldn't figure out how you ended up there, anyway."

"I'm learning how the big chains do it so I can be better prepared to open up an independent shop."

Cathy cracks a wide grin. "Why, Margaret Black. What a very sensible, non-impulsive thing to do. I'm impressed." She leans across the table. "But I'm not at all surprised. I'd have figured on you opening a coffee bar. I can't think of anyone more born to it than you. I think you'll be fabulous. We'll be there the minute you open the door."

I stare at Cathy. "I can't believe I was worried you'd hate the idea. I didn't sleep a wink last night wondering what I'd do if you laughed in my face."

"Come on now, we're family." She wraps me in a big hug. "I'd at least have the decency to laugh behind your back."

"Phase one complete!" I announce into my cell phone while I'm walking into Carter's to begin my shift.

"Brilliant," Will replies. "I told you she'd approve."

"Yeah, yeah, you and Diane were both right, I didn't need to worry, blah, blah, blah...but thanks for praying anyway. I could feel it."

"My pleasure. I've got a little surprise for you— to bolster up your spirits so you can talk to your parents. Can you come by the game tonight?"

"A surprise? Plus the opportunity to watch you hurl yourself at enormous sweaty men over a tiny leather ball? Who'd say no?"

I hear him chuckle over the phone and the sound sends tingles down my neck. "That tiny leather ball bashed your nose in. I wouldn't insult it if I were you. You know what they say about rugby."

I yank the door to Carter's open. "And what do they say about rugby?"

"That tennis is a game where thugs act like gentlemen, but rugby is a game where gentlemen act like thugs."

"All the more reason for me to come and ensure that all your thuggery stays on the field." I'm laughing to myself, picturing Will's teammates coming off the field to shrug their enormous shoulders into white dinner jackets. I've actually never seen anyone but Arthur off the field—who knows, the lot of them could clean up quite nicely. "See you tonight."

From the look on Nate's face, I must be grinning like a fool. He cracks a smile as he puts down a box of coffee filters. "Look at you," he says, thickening his accent to an outrageous degree. "It is worse than I thought. Come and tell Señor Fabulous all about the dashing *Ingles* who has stolen your finely caffeinated heart."

I tuck my handbag into the supply room. "You know, Nate, some days you're just plain scary. Friendly, funny, but scary." Nate is a wonderful guy. I can't for the life of me figure out why he's still single. *Hey God? Could You put the rush on finding him someone? He really deserves to be happy.*

"Don't be jealous *amigo*. Somewhere out there is a coffee-loving, God-fearing beauty just waiting to make *your* life complete." I tie my apron around my waist. I despise this silly apron. I'll never make my employees wear aprons. Ever.

Nate clutches his heart, still with the oversized accent. "Alone, I wait for her to grace my life with her fabulousness. Señor Fabulous was not meant for this aloneness."

Great. He's as theatrical as Diane. Just what I need in my life—more drama.

Wait a minute...

"We've got to work on that, *señor*. Come on, isn't there *anyone* who's come in here that you find appealing?"

"Have you seen any women walking in here with a Good Christian Single Woman name tag? The conversation hardly moves to theology with questions like 'do you want whipped cream on that?'"

"Ah," I say, pointing at him, "But 'do you want whipped cream on that?' is your specialty. If anyone could pull it off..."

Nate pulls a stack of cups out of the cabinet.

"Thanks for the compliment. I think that was a compliment. Was that a compliment?"

"That was a compliment. I'm serious. Wasn't there ever a customer who caught your eye?"

Nate stops and thinks. "There was one. Straight brown hair, shopping bags, went wild over the whipped cream thing. She was nice. A funny little laugh that stuck in your head all day. Great eyes."

I knew it! I don't know how I missed it before now: Diane. God is up in His heaven doubled over with laughter at this very moment, don't you think? So, do I tell him now? Or just move quietly behind the scenes to get the brunette back in here ASAP?

Opting for plan B, I wait a diversionary five minutes before I snag my cell phone out of my purse and send up a prayer of gratitude for the innovation of text messaging. I punch in Diane's number, followed by: *Carters. ASAP. B Cute!*

Chapter Twenty-Six

Something to do about it

"So Nate, with all the requisite apologies, I'd like you to meet my best friend Diane."

Nate looks understandably dumbstruck. "She. She's your best friend." He lets out a spurt of rapid-fire Portuguese under his breath. "The whole whipped-cream thing…"

"Was a setup. She didn't believe anyone could do it but me. I'm sorry about that. At least, I was sorry. Now I'm sort of…"

He waves off my chatter. "Forget it. I should feel sadly manipulated here, but instead I'm going to go with a strange sense of gratitude." Nate extends a hand. "Diane." He says the name like he's running his fingers through it.

"Nice to meet you, Nate. Maggie's told me a lot

about you." Diane looks slightly suspicious but mostly charmed.

"Can I pull you a drink? Tall hazelnut skim latte, right? And do you really like a 'smidge' of whipped cream, or was that just part of the act?"

Diane lets loose a dazzling smile. I told her to be cute, but she went beyond cute and well into stunning. "I don't like a smidge of anything. Yes, Nate, I'd like whipped cream on that. But let's keep the canister under control this time, hmm?"

"Whatever the lady wants." Nate starts to pull her drink, then stops to look at me. "She's your best friend. Her. The whole time."

I nod. Diane nods.

"You know, an ordinary man would find this highly disturbing."

I hand Nate the proper size cup for Diane's drink. "Good thing you're Señor Fabulous."

According to Will, they have this thing after games called a drink-up where everyone gets together. The girls who are invited, well, let's just say the average rugby player doesn't invite just *anyone* to the drink-up. As team captain, Will's presence is required at a drink-up—even if the game has been nasty. Like Will says, they may be thugs on the field, but they're perfect gentlemen when the game is over. He says it's a loud, friendly event, this time at the restaurant that sponsors Will's team. I've been invited to the game—and as such, to the drink-up. Which means my appearance is a declaration of sorts. So I'm guessing my surprise is my first official appearance as Will's...Will's what? Girl-friend? Date? Significant other? I hate those terms, but I don't suppose there's really an alternative out there.

By the time I get over there after work it's partway through the second half, so I take up a spot on a picnic table near the end of the field. They play for a while and I get a chance to see Will leading his team. You know how some people seem born to lead? As if it's in their blood, not their ambition? They have a natural sense of how to motivate people. They look them in the eye, they shoot straight and they pay respect when respect is due. I see all these things in how Will acts toward his team. I see bits of it in how he leads the class, but it really shows up in how he leads the team. Even though it feels like an odd sensation to have, I'm proud of him. I feel pleased and thankful that a man of his character has chosen a relationship with me. Is it becoming love for him as well? I think so, but I'm terrified to ask. I have a quiet sense that when it is, I'll know. He'll tell me. Imagine what that moment will be like. Will he be shy and stum-bling or dashing and chivalrous?

I'm lost in my romantic daydream when I realize the game is over and a burly man in a buzz cut is staring at me.

"Well, I'll be gobsmacked," he exclaims with a heavy cockney accent, kicking mud off his shoe.

Gobsmacked? Who comes up with these expressions? Granted, I've heard a lot worse from your average young male, but that one's so odd it's almost funny.

"Her!" our bulky young man comments, pointing a thick finger at me. "Your girl is that tiny thing Arthur bashed?" He gives Will a hearty slap on the back. "Well, why didn't you tell us all you had to do to get a girl to notice you was to let her bleed all over your team jersey? I'd have tried that months ago!"

"Maggie," says Will, reddening, "this enormous well-mannered beast is one of our forwards, Frank Smithwhite." My hand practically disappears inside the beefy hand Frank extends for a shake.

"Hello, sunshine!" Arthur calls out from the edge of the crowd with an atta-girl! look in his eye. I'm charmed by the idea that Will's been hanging back, waiting for the right woman, and that I'm her. It feels wildly wonderful.

It feels wildly public, too. Dirty faces are gaping at me. I'm blushing. It's like meeting a guy's parents, only weirder. There's fifteen of them and, believe me, they're the farthest thing from subtle about their assessment of me. I wouldn't be subjected to more scrutiny if I were up for sale on eBay.

"Finally get through to this *pommie,* did you?" Arthur grins, poking Will in the chest.

"So it would seem," I reply, feeling the blood surge up my neck.

"So it would seem indeed." Art gives me a wink. "'Bout time, too, if you ask me. Will's spent far too many drink-ups with no more than a Coke for company."

"Maybe now he'll give shorter speeches, eh?" Frank gives Will a nudge in the ribs that nearly knocks him over. Will didn't mention speeches. This should be interesting. We all sort of stare at each other for a moment, Will hanging oddly back, until Frank suddenly reaches into his pocket and steps toward me. "Well, 'bout time we take care of formalities."

Will's face takes on a panicked tone. "Frank, I've not…"

"'Course you 'aven't," says Frank, a wide smile on his face as he pulls a large strip of colored cloth out of his pocket. "Who would?"

"Who would what?" I stammer out, looking for any kind of a clue from Will. I grip the picnic table.

"Go easy on her, Frank…" Will says cautiously.

"Nonsense. She's here. She's coming to the drink-up she is. What more is there?"

"What's going on Will?" I scoot back further on the park bench.

Right into Arthur's hand, which wraps gently around my elbow as he catches the cloth Frank just tossed to him. "Just relax, sunshine, we won't hurt you. Mind your hair now." He blindfolds me with the cloth. "It's just a bit of *fun*." I am led off the table while some kind of ridiculous chant is yelled. "Arms up, love," Art says, and when I cautiously comply I feel a shirt or something pulled onto me. Whatever it is, it isn't clean—I can tell that much.

I hear lots of yelling around me and Will's laugh in the distance.

"Hang on, Maggie!" I hear him call. "I'm coming!"

A moment later, I feel a set of hands remove my blindfold. Will stands before me, grinning, clad in a brand new rugby shirt just like his old one, though with a crude, red paper heart pinned to the right sleeve.

He shrugs and grins at me. "Sorry about this."

I realize that the shirt I'm now wearing is the one Will wore in the game. It makes me smile. "You most certainly are not." Come on, you see the look on his face; he's not one ounce of sorry for this. He's enjoying this. As a matter of fact, he looks like he's waited his whole life for this.

I'm wearing a guy's dirty shirt.

And I'm on top of the world.

Just outside the restaurant, Will pulls me aside. He's positively glowing and nearly out of breath with all the nudging and kidding we've endured over the past twenty minutes. He fiddles with the paper heart. "You know, I rather knew they were going to do that. I just didn't expect them to get quite so hearty about it. You okay?"

Okay? I'm glowing. It sounds silly, but it feels wonderful to be known as "Will's girl." Sure, it has a goofy 1950s varsity-letter jacket mentality, but there's something genuinely satisfying about how happy Will's friends are for him. Will's trying hard to play it all down, but I can tell it means a lot to

him. Which is why it means a lot to me. "Sure," I
giggle. Yet another large hand reaches out to ruffle
Will's hair. I totally understand the roughhouse
style of affection—I've got a horde of brothers.

Thing is, Will has a horde of brothers, too. He
just hasn't figured it out yet.

"They're a bit rowdy," Will explains, "but they're
a grand bunch. They mean well." The crowd filters
inside, but Will hangs back. It's begun to rain,
cloaking the evening in darkness and mist. He takes
my hand and pulls me farther down the sidewalk,
ducking from awning to awning. He tugs us into the
small, covered entrance of a bookshop closed for the
evening. From its cozy shadows I hear the sputter-
ing sound of cars going by on the wet street. It's cool
and dark, but Will's eyes are gleaming. He fusses
with the shirt on me, rolling up the cuffs to find my
hands and hold them. He is such a handsome, gallant
man. How could I have ever thought him cold and
unfeeling? "Art's been waiting to shirt someone for
me for a long time, if you haven't noticed."

I smile, snuggling into the shirt. It smells like
him. I could freeze this moment in time and be
content for hours. "Your friends care about you.
They like seeing you happy."

"I am happy. I'm beyond happy." Will takes the
collar of his shirt and pulls me closer. "The other
night at practice, I missed four passes. Art pulled
me aside and, after cuffing me a few times, he said,
"What's the matter with ye, you clod, you in love
or somethin'?"

My entire nervous system slams into hyperdrive.

Will ducks his head until our foreheads are touching. "And I looked Art straight in his meddling, filthy face and said, 'As a matter of fact, I am.' I am in love with you, Maggie. I fell for you the minute you walked into my office."

I pull back, amazed. "You…fell for me…the first time we met?" I manage to spit out. From his expression, Will's either embarrassed or he's been bursting to say this for weeks—I'm not sure which.

He grins and my heart flutters. "Completely."

"Way back before class and the rugby pitch and even before that 'unwise given our situation' bit?"

He nods, one hand feathering the backs of his fingers across my cheek.

"All this time. And it took you *how* many weeks to give me any kind of encouragement while I was making a fool of myself over you?" I give him a playful little poke in the paper heart. "Hardly wearing your heart on your sleeve, hmm?"

"Well, for the sake of argument, I'd say it was the accident that truly did me in."

"Me? Bleeding all over you? Woozy on painkillers? That's the way to your heart?" Am I the only one who finds this disturbing?

"Apparently, yes. The whole damsel-in-distress-so-I-get-to-play-hero thing, I suppose. I'm as astounded as you are, believe me." He cups my face with his hands and my heart melts. "And there doesn't seem to be a thing I can do about it—or want to do about it."

My hands slide around his back. "Well, now, that would make two of us. I love you, too. I don't wear grungy shirts for just anyone, you know." Will's reply is a broad, radiant smile. "But you're sure there's nothing you want to do about it?" Zing, swoon, smitten—pick your descriptive and I'm already there.

"Well," Will says with a delicious tease to his voice, "I can think of at least one."

I lean in and close my eyes. *I'm way ahead of you, your lordship.*

Chapter Twenty-Seven

Desperation at the duck pond

Aww.

This is the gooey, sweet happy ending, right?

Sailing on the strength of our newfound love, Will and I put all the paperwork together and send me off to reveal my life's ministry to my parents, who stand instantly behind their brave little daughter and send me off to fulfill my ordained purpose.

The part where everybody sighs because boy loves girl, girl loves boy, innumerable obstacles have been overcome, God's in His heaven and all's right with the world.

So would you mind explaining what went wrong?

I'm not quite sure how I ended up here, sitting in my car outside the Seattle Asian Art Museum at Volunteer Park, staring at the duck pond.

Let me rephrase that. I know *how* I got here, I'm just not sure *why* I got here.

Will and I took my parents out to dinner this evening. Of course, I thought it would come as a surprise to them that we were—and I still can't quite hide my astonishment when I use these words—in love. Mom said she knew way back at the first dinner. That would be even before I knew it. Seems intuition isn't a life skill just for baristas— moms have it in spades. We told them about Higher Grounds and, true to Will's prediction, they were behind the idea with enthusiasm.

Will offered to stay with me as I told them about the loan part. Actually, he insisted on it. I wouldn't let him. For all my Maggie Bootstraps bravado, Diane was right—this time I needed to stand up on my own two feet. To stand on my faith and the sovereignty of my God. It's God who will make this work, not Will's protection or professionalism, even if he does play the hero exceedingly well.

So, I took a deep breath, parted ways with Will under some pretense (which really meant for him to go someplace and pray like crazy until I called) and went back to my parent's house for coffee. There, as boldly as I knew how, I laid out the financial details. I went through all the selling points, just like Will and I had rehearsed. I employed every bit of salesmanship I possess. I showed them spreadsheets and sales charts and even my mission statement. I wowed them. I could see, by the end of my presentation, that they understood my passion for the idea and the eternal value of it.

Which is why I nearly choked when they said no to cosigning the loan.

How could they say no? They're my parents, they love me, they want what's best for me and they say no?

They had all kinds of good, parental reasons. "I think you should do this thing," my father said, "but I won't put you—and your mother and I—into that kind of debt to make it happen."

"But Dad, it's my purpose, I *know* it is."

"I believe that," he said, grabbing my hand. "I'm sure this is your dream. But it's not ours. We have five children to see safely into the world, not just you. We have to think of that. And Maggie, so much debt? So young? You'd be so much better off saving up for this. If God wants it to happen, it will happen, when you're ready."

"But," I retorted, feeling like I'd heard way too many *no*s lately, "what if you *are* the way it's supposed to happen. I'm ready. I'll never be more ready. I can't get the loan without you."

"You are young and life is long," my mother replied, taking my other hand. I used to love it when she comforted me with that saying. It's what she would say when I was worried I'd never find what I wanted to do in life. Now I know exactly what I want to do and I hate the sound of the platitude.

Another set of *no*s.

Which means Higher Grounds could take years to happen.

Which means Stephen Markham could hand me the largest rejection in the history of banking. Or at least in *my* history of banking.

I cannot possibly see why God would allow this. Why give me the vision and then snatch it out of my hands?

I was sure I'd start sobbing the minute I left their house. Without even making a conscious decision to do so, I drove the car toward Volunteer Park and started up the hill. I kept waiting for the tears as my car wove its way up the winding road to the art museum parking lot, where you can see for miles. Do you remember the story of Abraham? God asks him to take his son Isaac and climb up the mountain to sacrifice him. Sacrifice this incredible blessing of a child that God had earlier promised him. To do this thing that seemed to destroy everything God had promised for Abraham's future.

I'm sitting here in my car in the art museum parking lot, waiting. Staring at those unsigned loan applications, hoping an angel will show up any second now to tell how it will all work out. *Really, Lord, now would be the ideal time to show me the far better plan You've got in the works.*

Nothing.

After half an hour of tearless emptiness, I do the thing I was supposed to do right away—I dial Will.

He answers the phone in one ring. Neither of us even bothers with "hello."

"They said no."

"I can't believe it." Shock pulls his voice tight.

"They won't cosign, Will."

"Let me talk to them. You said they'd say no the first time. They just need time to think it over. I can rerun a different payment schedule…"

"No," I interrupt him, "It won't change. They're dead against it. They didn't even like the idea of my taking out a loan, much less one big enough that I would need their help. I can't ask Mom and Dad to sign onto this loan again. They've given me their answer."

"Where are you?" I hear Will locking up his office in the background. He's coming for me.

"Outside the Asian Art Museum. The duck pond's really quiet this time of day."

"You mean at Volunteer Park? Up there?"

"Somehow I just sort of ended up here." I'm so tired all of a sudden. My arms and legs feel heavy with a surrendered sort of emptiness. An image which makes no sense.

"Stay there. I'll be there in twenty minutes. Ten."

For all my dislike of it, Will's overprotective-hero stuff would feel really good right now. I want to curl up in the shelter of someone more sensible. "Okay."

I find a bench and wait, praying and watching the ducks poke around on the pond. I realize I'm not calm at all. I'm quiet—an immovable sort of quiet, but it's more of a deer-in-headlights kind of frozen than it is anything approaching a calm.

"I simply cannot believe," he says as he bounds out of his car to hug me, "that God would bring you all this way, pull us together, place you in this class, *do all this,* only to have it go all wrong."

"You said it yourself—risk has costs and people get hurt."

He says nothing, just holds me very tight.

"You know," I say, trying to brighten my voice, "Markham could still say…yes." I barely get the *yes* out, the line feeling foolish. We both know the odds of approval now are painfully slim.

Will blows out a breath and we both sit down on the bench beside the pond. He stares up at the darkening sky. "I should have stayed with you. I think I could have convinced them."

"No, you couldn't have."

Will looks at me, "But they love you. They loved the idea. I saw their eyes light up when you told them about it. How could they say no to you?"

I suddenly realize this is how to explain my family. "That love you wondered about? The way we fight but still love each other? This is the same thing, I suppose." It clarifies itself right before my eyes, softening the disappointment even as I say the words. "Love isn't all yes and the opposite of love all no. We work it out with each other. We say what we mean, hold on to our opinions—even when they clash—and keep loving." An odd metaphor hits me and I erupt in a limp, sad giggle. "I was going to say it's not all black or all white, it's gray, but somehow that makes no sense since I'm Black and you're Grey and…" All my efforts to remain hopeful ball up into the back of my throat.

Will pulls me to his side, but I can't sit still. I have to fight the storm in the back of my throat or I'll drown.

"You know," I say, my words gaining speed as if running to keep ahead of the threatening tears, "I met this wonderful man who was so sure he could make my crazy dream line up into nice neat columns. But it won't. For a moment, you made me forget what a wild risk this was. And I realize, now, how much safer I felt when it was a wild, crazy, God-given risk. Then you started to make it real. You showed me how to build this risky vision into a real business. A solid business that could support my calling. You've done so much for me. I know so much more than I knew before."

"It was my privilege. My calling, even." He says, his own voice tight from my struggle.

"And those are good things. Good things are still in this. We have to keep looking for the good things." I'm talking myself out of the gloom now, pacing as if the disappointment is stalking me from behind. "It looks bad. It looks really, really bad. But it's not over until Markham says no, right? It's not truly over until he gives me an answer. So I've got to keep going, don't I?"

I look at Will, but he doesn't say anything.

"I mean, there's a difference between risk and foolishness. There's a difference between the plan that can't work and God's plan you can't see. God is in the habit of asking people to risk failure all the time." I begin ticking risky Bible business off on my fingers, still pacing. "Noah building an ark, Abraham, Mary, that prophet guy who made the starving woman use her last bit of food to feed him, Peter stepping out of the boat to walk on water...."

Will stands up, baffled. "You never give in and you never give up, do you Maggie Black?"

"I'm trying. I don't have a lot to go on here."

He catches me at the end of another paced lap and says the one thing I need to hear most.

"Who knew I'd love you most of all when you don't have a leg to stand on?"

"Yeah," I say, giving into the strength of his embrace. "I'm thinking that's pretty much how it looks."

Chapter Twenty-Eight

Ten whole seconds

Will was right, you know.

I *am* Maggie Bootstraps and I don't go down without a fight. Sure, the odds are wildly against me. But you know me. I grit my teeth, brew a double-shot latte and dig in for the uphill climb.

I stayed in class and fine-tuned my business plan. I submitted my loan application last Thursday, just like everybody else. I'm braced for impact, but I'm not dead in the water yet. It's Monday and Will presented every application to the loan board at 10:00 a.m. today, with his approval or rejection.

Except for mine, of course, which I presented to Steve Markham at 11:00 a.m.

I bought a fabulous new handbag for the occasion. I brought coffee. I brought mock-ups of menus and ads, photos of the espresso machines. I focused every ounce of salesmanship I possess on Steve Markham.

Stephen J. Markham, vice president of lending, according to his business card. He had the meanest office I'd ever seen—not even a family photo to break up the gray, corporate callousness. An unbelievably serious guy in an unbelievably serious suit. He looked as though he scraped small businesses off his shoes before he went home at night.

He just kept listening, silent as a statue, flipping through the business plan as I walked him through it. The man could be a robot; his face was that emotionless.

I got two words out of him the entire hour: "Good coffee."

I was shooting for "yes, approved."

It's looking bad. Very bad. Still, if God can move mountains, God can move Steve Markham. I've said that over and over to myself as I wait on a park bench outside the bank. The only humane thing about the whole process is Markham agreeing to let Will convey the bank's answer.

It was Will's idea and was perhaps the greatest act of love I have ever known.

Will walks out of the bank, slow and erect. He's hated every single second of this and I know that. I love him for sticking it through.

My goal was ten seconds. I make it. Ten whole seconds pass between the moment Will shakes his head and the moment I burst into tears.

What does Will do? He lets me cry all over his suit jacket, even after he handed me his handkerchief. "I have a friend at the bank who says, 'I don't get paid to say yes. Saying yes is wonderful. I get paid to say no because saying no is work.' This particular no is excruciating."

"Yeah, well, saying it beats hearing it, I can tell you."

"Not by much. I hate this, Maggie. Can I just put that on the record? I hate every single bit of this."

"I know." And I do. Will tucks my shoulder under his arm. I notice it looks like it's going to rain soon and I decide it's fitting. My dreary day should have dreary weather. We're both silent for a moment. Will's hand strokes my arm and he leans down and plants a couple of quiet kisses on the top of my head.

I lost.

I fought and fought with everything I had and I lost Higher Grounds. At least for now.

It aches like someone shot a cannon through my chest.

After a time, Will catches my chin with his free hand and looks into my eyes. "You put up a brave, fine battle and I love you for it. I love you for taking it on and seeing it through. For dreaming such a big, impossible plan. You make this whole business enormously complicated, do you know that? I'm supposed to love some nice, sweet, compliant little British thing who puffs up my male ego. Instead, I get you overhauling my insides and tackling huge tasks and making no sense at all."

"I make all kinds of sense," I reply, feeling a tiny bit lighter. "I just don't make *your* kind of sense." I settle back onto Will's shoulder, letting out a huge, shuddering sigh.

"What are you going to do now?"

That's the question of the hour, isn't it? The rain begins to fall and we take a moment to listen to the soothing sound from under the awning where we are. I absentmindedly fold his handkerchief into a neat little square on my lap. What am I going to do now? After another sigh, I give the only answer I have. "I have absolutely no idea."

"You're not going to go off and build an ark or anything, are you?"

"No," I giggle, poking him.

"Not going to attempt a parting of Puget Sound, not going skulking off to some foreign dignitary asking him to 'Let my people go,' or go marching around Portland seven times blasting any trumpets?"

"No," I say, laughing openly now.

"You're not going to tell me I ought to start composing Hail Margarets or that we have seven years of feast and famine on the way or that I should keep a sensible distance between you and all slingshots when surrounded by angry Philistines?"

I'm laughing *and* crying now. It feels horrible and very freeing at the same time.

"Because you see, I'm quite sure I've reached my tolerance level for risk. For the entire decade perhaps. I'm going to have to be excruciatingly sensible for at least two years in order to recover.

This hideous love business. Hits without any warning whatsoever. There ought to be an alarm or some such thing." He wraps his arms around me and I drink in how good it feels. "Margaret Black, I wish I understood you as much as I loved you."

"Ah, William," I say, adopting a sorry version of his accent. "Where'd be the fun in that?"

Chapter Twenty-Nine

Ain't that always the way?

I didn't bounce back right away.

I didn't expect to, but it still seemed to surprise a few people. It's not like I wanted to crawl inside a gallon of chocolate sauce and be alone with my misery, but I wasn't really in a social kind of mood. Will and I took a few long walks, but mostly I kept to myself, prayed and filled half a journal trying to figure out what to make of the whole thing.

I quit Carter's, too. Without a new job lined up.

My manager looked utterly shocked. I can't even remember the reason I made up for leaving. Why did I really leave? Good question. There seem to be a dozen answers. It hurt, actually, to be slinging someone else's coffee when it didn't feel like a stepping stone on the way to slinging my own. And

I knew, somehow, that I'd learned all I could from that place.

So I took a few weeks off. Spent time with my family. Made lots of hot chocolate for Charlie and helped his family paint a room for the new baby. It was nice being around all that newness and possibility when it felt like so many doors were shutting tight for me.

I don't know how to wait. I don't even know if I'm supposed to be waiting. I know who I was before Higher Grounds, but I can't go back to being her. And I can't have Higher Grounds—at least not yet.

So who am I in between?

"I thought I'd find you here," Will comes scrambling up the path to where I'm sitting on the back of the Fremont troll's concrete VW Beetle. I've spent quite a few afternoons with the troll lately. I feel an odd solidarity with him, stuck here in his concrete corner with his concrete car, waiting for a second car that will never come his way. All the cars are far above his head, far out of his reach. And yet, he's right where trolls ought to be—under a bridge. That's how I feel: right where I ought to be, but with what I really want far out of my reach.

Will hoists himself up beside me, sliding off his tie and kissing the top of my head. "Come up with anything yet?" You guessed it, Will's given me the assignment of making a list of what I'd like to do now. It's not working any better than the other lists he had me do.

"I just keep coming up with *wait*. And I hate waiting. I don't want to wait. I can't afford to wait long. Nancy Chang's flower shop is looking pretty good right now if she'll take me back." I show him my decidedly blank journal page.

"Would you go back?"

"I don't think I can go back. It was easy to work there when I didn't know what I wanted to do with myself. Now, it just feels like a substitute. But so would Carter's." I heave a sigh. "So would anything. Anything that isn't Higher Grounds isn't anything."

Will smirks. "And I always read being in love made people more optimistic. Well, looks like I picked the right day for my present to you." He pulls an envelope out of his jacket pocket and hands it to me. "Actually it's not much of a present. Or it's a present to both of us." He groans, "I still make no sense around you. But here you are anyway. I think you'll like it. It's your doing."

I have no idea what to expect. I open the envelope to find a bill. A telephone bill, to be exact. Someone needs to work on his gift-giving skills. Bills I have enough of—I'm unemployed, remember? There's one international call, highlighted in yellow. It's a forty-seven minute call to Italy from Will's apartment. Calling to see if they'll hire me as the spokesmodel for La Marzocco espresso machines, maybe? Who says I've lost my optimism?

"That," Will says, pointing to the highlighted item, "is a phone call to none other than William Grey Jr."

It takes me a moment to catch his meaning. When I do, Will smiles a shaky, almost impish grin. "Will," I say softly, "you spoke to your dad?"

"For forty-seven whole minutes."

I'm stunned. He's right on two counts: 1) it's an odd present and 2) I like it very much. "What did you say to him?"

Will pulls one knee up and wraps an arm around my shoulders. "I told him," he says softly, laying his head on top of mine, "that I met someone. That I'm in love with her and that part of the reason I love her is the great big dreams she has. I told him you would probably like each other very much and that I would call him again sometime soon."

I twist around to catch his eye. "It took you forty-seven minutes to say all that?"

"We are British. Not very direct, you know."

I kiss his hand and settle further into his embrace. "How do you feel? About it and all?"

Will thinks for a moment. "Odd. A bit sad, a bit hopeful, a bit of everything. But better all the same. It's like the rose thorns I used to prick myself on in Mom's garden. It hurts a bit, but the thorn's gone." He laughs softly, "When did I start talking like you? Silly metaphors and all?"

"Whazza matter, sunshine?" I say, adopting Art's cockney with less-than-perfect results. "You in love or somethin'?"

"Very much so," Will says, pulling me closer. "Very much so."

* * *

Mom, Dad and I are okay. It was awkward there for a week or two, but they did what they always have done; they kept on loving me until it worked itself out. But some things are different now. Mom keeps trying to get Will to eat more—that's entertaining. And Charlie keeps making Will say *ginger hair* and read his Dr. Seuss books—*Green Eggs and Ham* is hilariously ironic with a British accent.

One benefit to quitting Carter's—besides not having four loads of white laundry every week—is not seeing so much of Nate. I get enough gooey happiness from Diane. And now the two are head-over-heels about each other. Granted, Diane falls in love faster than soldiers fall in line, but this time it looks like it might stick. I'm happy for her. It's a sickening, oh-will-you-two-cut-it-out sort of happy, but I'm happy for her just the same. I did ask God to send her a boyfriend pronto, after all.

Tonight's the night we all knew was inevitable: the double date. Actually, I'm amazed it hasn't happened until now. Will and I are meeting Diane and Nate for dinner.

It sounded like a good idea at the time, but I'm regretting it already. They're awfully lovey-dovey—as Will puts it—and I'm feeling stuck in sulk-mode today.

"It won't be all that bad," Will consoles me as we get out of his car. "You'll enjoy yourself."

I look down the street to see Diane and Nate running—actually running—down the street hand in hand. Looking nearly giddy. "Yikes," I mutter. Oh, this was a bad idea, even if she is my best friend.

"Nonsense," Will says, attempting a wave. "They're cute in a sugary, excessive kind of way." He's trying very hard to put a good spin on things. "It'll be lovely, really." Now even Will sounds unconvinced.

He should be. If you could see the wall of supreme joy barreling down Broadway at us this very moment, you might have the same urge to run for your life I'm currently stifling. They just came from Nate's Bible study, for crying out loud, no one should be that bubbly.

Diane skids to a halt in front of us, her eyes wide. She makes a quick, breathless set of introductions between Will and Nate, who shake hands even though they've already met twice. "Mags," she says, taking my shoulders, "you have to come with us. Now."

"What?"

"Now. You have to come with me, with us."

"Where?"

"Nate's Bible study is just over and if you don't hurry he'll be gone. Just come, we'll explain it all when we get there." With that, the two lovebirds grab hands and start back up the block the way they came.

Will looks at me. I look at Will. Suddenly, Diane doubles back and yanks my hand. "I mean NOW!"

Broadway's a pretty creative street. You'll likely see all kinds of things walking down the block. But two pairs of grown adults sprinting? That's gotta draw stares.

Nate and Diane push through the doors of a church, pulling us through a maze of corridors to a pretty little study where the aforementioned Bible study seems to be just breaking up.

"Dawson! You're still here! Excellent." Nate pulls a snazzy looking older gentleman to his feet, planting him in front of Will and me.

"Maggie Black, this is Dawson Bentley." Nate says it like I should know the name. It sounds vaguely familiar, but I can't quite place it. Nor can I imagine why it is so urgent I make his acquaintance.

"Pleased to meet you Maggie," Dawson says, his voice dripping in a broad southern drawl. "Nate here's been goin' on about you."

"Good, I hope?" I say, staring at Nate, who's currently doubled over in an attempt to catch his breath.

"Mighty fine."

Diane chimes in, looking like she's about to burst. "Dawson owns the Bent's Brew coffeehouse in Queen Anne, Maggie."

Now I know why the name seemed familiar. It's a very nice coffee joint. But I'm really not in the market for mentors right now.

"More importantly," Nate gasps, straightening up, "Dawson just told us that he's thinking of selling the place. He's retiring."

"I'm done with retail for now. Gonna go spend

some time in China doing mission work with my two nephews. Ain't got no kids of my own and neither one of those two rascals seems interested in brewin' coffee for a living."

Things just got interesting. Wouldn't you agree?

"Maggie, would you believe Dawson was just sitting here offering up a prayer request for the right person to come and take over his shop?"

Okay, things just got really, *really* interesting.

"Let me rephrase that—the right Christian person? One who would turn that location into a Christian coffeehouse?"

My pulse has halted. I feel Will grab my hand.

"This town needs another java joint like it needs a hole in the head. What it don't have, near as I can tell, is a coffee place with *soul*. With faith. Nate here tells me you've got it in your head to pull something like that off."

I open my mouth, but don't seem to be able to string any words together.

"Indeed she does," Will pipes in with his banker voice suddenly on. "I've read her five-year business plan. But, well, financing has been…an issue."

"Ain't that always the way. Which is why I was just mentioning how I'd be willing to turn the place over on a lease-to-own basis. To the right person with the right plan, of course."

Nate grins.

Diane beams.

I pounce. "Oh, I've got plans all right."

"They're sound," Will adds.

"If you can scrape together enough of a down payment, little lady, I might even be interested in offerin' private financing myself. Kids are expensive enterprises, so not havin' 'em makes it easy to set aside a little cash over the years."

Now would be a very poor time to faint. Breathing, however, is becoming a bit of a challenge. Nate and Diane have just become the most adorable couple on the planet. Will's eyes are saucers and his hand is so tight on mine I think it's the only thing holding me upright.

Will clears his throat. "Just out of curiosity, Mr. Bentley, what type of espresso machines are in the shop?"

"La Marzoccos, young man. I believe in having the best equipment you can get your hands on. Got two of 'em, as a matter of fact—one for the drive-through and one for the counter business."

"Their own advertisement, those machines are," Will says, smirking at me.

"Hey, you know your stuff, mister."

I put out my hand, feeling like I am reaching into my future. "Mr. Bentley, are you free for dinner?"

Epilogue

Three little words

"I love you" are the three most precious words in the English language. On either side of the Atlantic.

"Open for business," however, come in a very close second.

I can hardly believe I'm standing behind my coffee counter, running my machines, brewing up my coffee.

In my shop.

It's been six weeks and I haven't stopped grinning yet. I may never stop grinning. There isn't a joy more complete in the entire world than doing exactly what you're supposed to be doing, in exactly the right place with exactly the right people. I feel God smiling down on me every minute of every day.

Cathy and the new baby come in every Tuesday for story hour. You haven't lived until you've heard

Nate read *The Very Hungry Caterpillar.* Yep, I hired Nate. I think some of the moms may come in just to hear his accent, but you'll never hear me admit that out loud.

We hosted a fundraiser for our church clothing ministry the other night, put on by the women's Bible study that meets here Thursday evenings. My brother's band didn't do too badly with the music. They might make it after all, even though Mom says she can't understand a word they're singing.

The back sink broke last week, but it wasn't enough to throw off my repair and maintenance budget for the quarter. I can almost do my own computerized bookkeeping without Will looking over my shoulder now.

Remember Bea Haversham? Grandma Biscuits from Will's office? She came in shortly after we opened. We had a delightful lunch together while we planned a retirement brunch for someone at the bank. They've never done it off-site before, but Bea is one persuasive lady when she sets her mind to something. I think she takes personal credit for Will and I—and I can't say I really mind. You could do a lot worse than having Bea Haversham in your corner.

We had a class reunion of sorts here two weeks ago and Will was practically bragging about my cash-flow projections to Josh, Jerry, Linda and all the people from entrepreneur school. Well, at least I think he was bragging. It's hard to tell under all that adorable British reserve.

* * *

Speaking of British reserve, I forgot to mention the secret specialty of the house: the Limey Latte.

Don't get your hopes up—it's an ordinary cup of Earl Grey tea. Done to perfection, of course.

Will comes in for one every day on his way to work.

* * * * *

Dear Reader,

Coffee and tea are like life: common yet rare, simple yet complex, familiar yet filled with things still to learn. Maggie and Will discover life's imperfections and bumps in ordinary settings, but they prove the truth that life—even at its most familiar—is never ordinary. Wonders hide under the mundane, and love hides where we least expect it.

Maggie and Will teach each other that life never runs in a straight line. The twists and turns are God's classroom, where He sends events and people to further shape us into citizens of the Kingdom. Some of life's journeys are easier than others, but the journey itself can always be trusted *if* we recognize God's sovereignty. The "delightful inheritance" promised us in Psalm 16 is always secure.

Stop by www.alliepleiter.com and share a digital visit, or send a note to me at P.O. Box 7026, Villa Park, IL 60181 and share your thoughts.

Blessings,

QUESTIONS FOR DISCUSSION

1. Have you ever had a dream like Maggie's Higher Grounds? Could you see God in the plan? How has your life changed because of that dream?

2. Maggie wants to get started on her dream right away. When is it good to jump into an idea, and why is it sometimes wise to wait? What are you dying to jump into and why?

3. Will chose to put distance between himself and his family problems. Do you agree with his choice? How would you respond in a similar situation?

4. Not everyone would think of coffee as a ministry. What ordinary gift do you have that God could use in a surprising way?

5. Will and Maggie argue over faith vs. facts. Where has that issue risen in your life? Where did you place your trust and why?

6. Do you agree with Maggie's parents' decision? How would you have responded to the same request?

7. Is your family more like Will's or Maggie's? How has that affected how you see the world?

8. Share a time when something silly, like Maggie's whipped cream trick, brightened your day. Can you set out to do something like that, or does it have to happen spontaneously to really work?

9. When has God "taken something away" only to "give it back" to you in an even better way? How can that strengthen your faith for tough times?

10. Maggie talks about "life happening over coffee." Who do you need to share a cup with (be it tea or coffee or whatever)? Is there someone God might be nudging you to connect—or reconnect—with? Share your ideas and make some plans.